PENGUIN BOOKS

My Brother Tom

 James Aldridge was born in White Hills, Victoria and attended Swan Hill High School. He began his career as a copyboy and then worked in the Picture Library of the Melbourne *Sun*.

In 1938 he went to London and worked as a newspaperman on the *Daily Sketch*. During the war he became a war correspondent in Finland, Egypt and then the Soviet Union working for the Australian Newspaper Service, the North American Newspaper Alliance of New York and also for *Time* and *Life*.

James Aldridge's first novel was written during the war when he was a journalist. After the war he decided to leave regular journalism to have more time for his novels. He has lived in the United States, London and Europe, with two long visits home to Australia. His wife is Egyptian and they have two sons.

James Aldridge has written twenty-three novels, many of them set in Australia. He is probably best known in Australia for *A Sporting Proposition* which was made into the film *Ride a Wild Pony*, and for his recent award-winning novel, *The True Story of Lilli Stubeck*.

Also by James Aldridge

My Brother Tom

James Aldridge

Penguin Books

Penguin Books Australia Ltd,
487 Maroondah Highway, P.O. Box 257
Ringwood, Victoria, 3134, Australia
Penguin Books Ltd,
Harmondsworth, Middlesex, England
Penguin Books,
40 West 23rd Street, New York, N.Y. 10010, U.S.A.
Penguin Books Canada Limited,
2801 John Street, Markham, Ontario, Canada, L3R 1B4
Penguin Books (N.Z.) Ltd,
182-190 Wairau Road, Auckland 10, New Zealand

First published 1966 by Hamish Hamilton
Published in Penguin, 1979
Reprinted 1986

Offset from the Penguin 1979 edition
Made and printed in Australia by
The Dominion Press–Hedges & Bell

Aldridge, James, 1918-
My brother Tom.

ISBN 0 14 004580 5 (pbk.).

I. Title.

A823'.3

For William and Thomas

Author's Note

It is true that my parents were English and that I was brought up in an Australian country town, but my father was not a lawyer and I had no younger brother, nor have any of the events I portray here in the name of my father and mother anything to do with my family at all, nor are any of the other people any part of reality. 'I' am the narrator simply as a fictional device which permits concision and a great deal of elbow room.

I

I meant to begin this account of the summer of 1937–1938 with the problem which my wife Eileen and I face now with our seventeen-year-old son. Then I planned to get down to the real point of it which is not my son at all but my younger brother Tom, who was seventeen twenty-seven years ago in a small bush town in Australia. I wanted above all to reveal the huge difference between a boy emerging now into young manhood and a boy emerging then, so that I could explain what has happened to my generation in the period between. But I wonder already if the point is worth making.

We are no longer an admirable generation, that seems clear. Though we did fight in the war, we simply fell apart when a handful of frightened men cried treason at us after the war. We abandoned too easily what we knew was right, yet the values we had acquired in our youth are just as good now as they were then, only we failed to hand them on. This view of our lives is important, because the story of my brother Tom is partly one of moral hindsight. Tom was always at war on the frontiers of hope, whereas my adolescent son Dick is struggling today with a world that is far too directionless to have much of a hopeful aim to it.

Eileen doesn't see it quite the same way. I approach these two boys (so far apart) with the sort of moral and social and political outlook that I think is lacking now, but Eileen is so practical that to her all ideologies, even those she believes

9

in, are mere curtains which hide the best part of life. We have unpleasant quarrels about this.

Dick himself, just beginning to burst gaudily into full-feathered manhood, is like Eileen not like me. He looks like her, he thinks like her, he teases life the way she does with bold bright eyes, and the result is a stand-up fight between them on almost every step of the way: it might begin with an unwiped bathtub and then reach fury sometimes over the rudeness and the ignobility of modern adolescent behaviour. Yet morally they are inseparables.

What *I* see as the real pitfall for him is the lack of any real ideology. There is only survival and affluence now, nothing much else. But Eileen doesn't worry about that; instead she looks at the sexual slaughterhouse of the 1960s and shudders, and she is prepared to say to her son that if he ever gets a girl into trouble he will have to marry her. She is sure that he won't, because she knows her own character so she knows his, but this is partly the practical measure she has of the problem he faces. We are, in fact, taking exactly the same view of it, only our interpretations of the moral threat are different.

I therefore tell the story of my brother Tom to unashamedly make a point. I suppose it is principally a love story, taking everything else into account. Perhaps there are other closer parallels to what is happening now, perhaps not. The locale at least is different, because there is nothing similar in the black wet London street I live in now and in that pleasantly dry and faintly dusty Australian bush town, placid in its summer shell of white shade from the stringy eucalypts and peppercorn trees lining its main street. It was a far away place then, but we escaped nothing of the world's agony by its remoteness.

2

would with the living agony of the earth in their spinal columns. In the moonlight, under the bird whip, waited desperately through a Roman convict's night while heaven-throated men were mad or dying as again I wandered these spinal journeys of pallid stone and a whimper that had to be caught, an escapade I had felt long ago suddenly that we could not

St Helen was the railhead and market town for a local farming area the size of an English county, and it lay low on the Victorian side of the River Murray, hooked to a ten-mile bend in the river which formed a swampy island in winter we called the Billabong. The Murray River to us was what the Scamander was to the Trojans, although our pagan gods were not the golden shadows of our dead heroes but the big farmers whose kingdom was the wide flat wheat-lands which, after harvest in December, became a dusty mess. The natural mallee scrub which had once held the earth to the earth had been rolled down by land-hungry squatters and settlers, and now the summer winds blazed across the bare plains each year and took the crest off the earth in blinding dust-storms. Our rich red valley was, in fact, being worked to death.

But the town looked prosperous even in the thirties when almost every young man in it was unemployed and when all the money was in the banks or in the vast red debits of domestic debts, but nowhere else. We were all borderline cases, and respectable people in the town were nearer hunger, surrounded by a million acres of ripe wheat, than anyone liked to admit. But everything in that area had to pass through the town to the city, not only the wheat and wool and mutton, but dried grapes and oranges from up river, lettuces and tomatoes from the river valley, butter from the butter factory and beef from the slaughter-yards. As a boy, lying awake on the verandah where I slept, I would hear the baying agony of the cattle in the early morning being led to the slaughter, and years later when I walked dazedly through a Russian-German battlefield where fourteen thousand men were dead or dying in agony I remembered those painful mornings of animal pain, and it was years after that before I could eat meat again. I had realized quite suddenly that we eat death.

We had four schools – one Catholic, two State schools (which were excellent) and a private and expensive girls' school where my sister Jean (15) went. We had five lawyers (including my father), five doctors, a local newspaper on which I went to work, eight pubs (hotels), five banks and three private aeroplanes, one the property of another local 'barrister and solicitor' who had been an ace in the First World War. The social rules for the town's behaviour were written by its shopkeepers; the lawyers and doctors and chemists were its decorative gentry; and the big sheep farmers from the Riverside stations and the big wheat farmers along the plains were the aristocracy, no less feudal for their easy-going link with the rest of the town.

My English father, Edward J. Quayle, had arrived in St Helen from the gold-mining town of Bendigo in Victoria, and before that he had come from New Zealand and before that Natal, Karachi, British Honduras and among other places Budleigh Salterton where he was once deacon, or vicar, I'm not sure which. But he had left the church somewhere else in the world before he reached Australia and taken a law degree in his thirties and became what is called in Australian an 'amalgam' – a mixed barrister and solicitor who is allowed to practise both professions of the law in Victorian country towns. Temperamentally he was another and more incompatible mixture of bigoted Victorian moralist and uncompromisingly romantic lawyer, and he could never solve the difference.

But there was nothing small in him. Spiritually he leaned a great deal on Bishop Berkeley, but his romantic alter-egos were Walter Pater, Anatole France and Ruskin-Gothic. He was short and hot-tempered and violently convinced that he was right, and I knew that if he had parted company with the Church it was not because of some moral disagreement with the commandments, but because he had been right and some church official had been wrong. He still argued dogma with the local Anglican priest but never went to Church although we had to. He argued with the town councillors about the roads or the rights of way, or with the police about the drunkenness on Saturday nights, and he was on bad terms with every circuit judge in whose courts he argued his cases. My father was always presenting a case, even in ordinary conversation, yet it was more often than not a case which only God himself could really judge properly. He was therefore less a lawyer than a moral fundamentalist who simply wanted to put the town straight, a fascinated moral advocate who lived for his right to interpret. Everything else was more or less a waste of time which is probably where both Tom and I got our strong moral streak from.

This isn't a harsh judgement of my father; it is simply the way he was and the way he influenced our lives. He was also generous and clever and cultured. He knew English literature thoroughly and thought Marlowe's *Faust* better than anything Shakespeare ever wrote (I was named after Marlowe), and he never bore a grudge although he believed in punishment. He was really Manx and proud of his family name and its Viking associations, and he was a fighter. He fought that whole hostile Australian town with its own favourite weapons – contempt and ridicule. I think he had come to Australia, like so many Englishmen, imagining himself to be the superior force, and nothing he found in

Australia had changed his mind. So they not only ridiculed him in the town for his English sense of superiority – his claim to be the lawgiver, they laughed at his moral interference in *their* lives, and he reciprocated with his contempt for any and every native Australian institution, no matter what it was. He had once pinned a notice to his office door which said that anybody who could not pronounce properly simple English words like 'street', 'bone' and 'day' and phrases like 'I don't know' need never come into his office again. He was fed up with a saturation of Australian 'straits' and 'boans' and 'dais' and 'ai dunnos'. That night someone sliced down all my gentle mother's standard English roses in the front garden, which made her dislike the town even more than she normally did, and my mother, unlike my father, was not given to hate and morality and fighting.

This sort of behaviour kept us poor, because only the desperate would come to him, only those who couldn't afford one of the other lawyers who didn't antagonize the justices and the magistrates. In reality he was a very good lawyer, he knew his law better than the other barristers and solicitors in the town, often better than the judges, and what we managed to live on financially was the recognition of his talents by outsiders, such as city insurance companies and farm implement manufacturers who were always suing some small farmer for non-payment.

I never fought anyone who ridiculed my father, because I learned early to compromise with Australian mockery and I often laughed at him with the rest of the town; but my brother Tom, who always resented him as a boy (though I didn't) fought countless tough little fights over him at school, or rather over the inevitable position we were put into by his way with the town. I once saw Tom, aged ten, hit a professional provocateur in our midst, aged twelve, for calling the old man 'mudface'. The words were not even out of Mike Mitchell's mouth when Tom in a fury swished his two hands, laced together by the fingers, and knocked little Mitchell silly. But this was typical anyway, because Tom who was small and blond and built like a little stallion would fight for his honour on an instant. He was always being trapped into violence by his indignation. And yet you could see in his rather feminine blue eyes that the whole idea of violence always repelled him, even as a boy, although he fought his way up fiercely through most of the boys in the town.

3

On the surface Tom went on growing up wild, but perhaps I was the only one then who knew his secret. I knew how much he suffered for his impulsiveness and recklessness, because I suppose we Quayles all suffered alike with our protestant consciences. But Tom's conscience didn't bother to keep him out of trouble. At school he instinctively broke windows. He once set fire to two hundred acres of dry grass near our house, accidentally, of course, when he was burning off grass in preparation for Guy Fawkes (November is summer out there). He got a terrible hiding for that. He had once, somehow, put a six-foot black snake (poisonous) alive through my mother's old-fashioned mangle because he wanted to flatten it out to make a snake-belt. I remember the black, bloody stain on the wooden rollers years afterwards. He had once climbed to the top of the local radio transmitting mast, a long wooden pole about a hundred feet high, to tie an insulator to a guy rope which had fallen – payment five shillings. The mast had swayed dangerously back and forth and half the street had collected, holding their breaths, until he had climbed safely down. He had been caught, aged ten, stealing bottles from the back of the local soft-drink factory and taking them around to the front to sell for a penny each, and the factory owner, Issie Sion, had sensibly kicked his behind and let him go. He had run away from home twice, and both times had spent the night over the river on the Billabong, fishing and trapping rabbits. My mother had been sick with worry, yet she had a profound confidence in Tom's ability to survive everything, and Tom knew it. He had been brought home each time and given a 'sound thrashing' by my father and sent to bed. Tom took his hidings dry-eyed and unresentfully, but I knew he wept to himself afterwards at the injustice of it all. When my father whacked me I yelled as loud as I could after the first blow and escaped the worst, but I had learned to compromise early the way Tom never did.

Yet that other Tom, with a conscience like a bushfire, was always kicking himself for his wickedness and thoughtlessness, and the time I write about here is the summer of 1937-38 when his fighting and childishly easy days were over and he was trying to bring the two parts of himself together – the wild and wicked part, and the conscientious and gentle one. Life, in fact, was just being felt by the fingertips, he was just becoming aware, and the first thing he recognized as a problem was the fact that our egalitarian Australian town was out to flatten him and everybody else into nothing at all if it could.

By that summer Tom had already gone as far as he could in the local High School. He had decided unhesitatingly that he wanted to be a lawyer, although he had no hope of getting to university because we could not afford it. So my father took him (unpaid) into his office 'for the summer', a temporary solution taken desperately as if everybody hoped that *something* would turn up to give Tom a chance when the annual season of mellow fruits and golden harvests was over.

Tom knew he had very little chance. He was a naturally clever boy, but so far he had been happily burning himself up and was therefore not in an academic position to win one of the very rare scholarships to Melbourne University, and only the country rich could send their sons to college otherwise. I had already been through this disembodiment myself, although I must admit I had never had much desire to go to university at all. I had always wanted to be a newspaperman on a city paper, but I had no qualifications for it, and anyway there were no jobs in the city for country boys, or for city boys for that matter, so I had pestered the owner of our local *Standard*, a sympathetic old lady named Royce who gave me a temporary chance also – one year. I had been out of work for two years after leaving school, drifting through a dozen temporary roles, and this job was a miracle, even though it would only last a year and I would be paid less than a pound a week.

I suppose I should have been romantically satisfied, but the future outlook then was too hopeless to be too happy about anything, in fact my social senses were scarred for life by the dead end we all faced in those days. In 1937 the depression was by no means over, in fact even up till 1939 thousands of men on the wallaby who were looking for seasonal work in the neighbouring countryside passed through our town. Someone slept on the dirt floor of our garage almost every week, summer and winter. If they were Australian my father would send Tom out to them with hot water for tea and bread and jam (no butter, we often could not afford it ourselves) and if they were English immigrants of any age or duration my father would inspect them and if they were respectable enough he would sometimes invite them up for one meal with the family. Tom would secretly talk bloody revolution to them, but I was afraid of them because I knew they hated our charity and my father's lengthy grace. Only the poor tolerated the swaggies, the rich (like me) were afraid of them and hated them.

Not only rich and poor divided the town on differences of this sort, but farmers and townspeople divided it on their difference, the sporting-betting-drinking crowd and the unsporting-unbetting-undrinking crowd divided it; but the simplest and most effective division was that of Protestant and Catholic.

This was absolute, a division which my father considered essential to the honour and faith you could feel for a fellow man. To him, all Roman Catholics were untrustworthy, disloyal and self-seeking to the point of cynicism; they were moral outsiders. My father believed literally in the Reformation, and *now*, because it had freed Englishmen to think as they pleased. The combination of Australia and Catholic was unbearable to my father, but the combination of Australian and Catholic *and* the sporting-betting-drinking crowd like the MacGibbon family was nothing less than destructive and disastrous.

And Tom carelessly fell in love that summer with Margaret MacGibbon whose father, Lockie MacGibbon, was the town's showman, speculator, boxing promoter, gambler and Catholic mocker of the Protestant bigotry and English snobbery personified by my father; and the unusual relationship which Tom's carelessness brought to our two families began with a fire that burned Lockie MacGibbon's house to the ground.

4

It was always a miserable experience to watch one of the houses in the town burn down, because we all knew each other so well. Almost all houses in St Helen were made of wood and were roofed with corrugated iron and the whole town lived in fear of fire. The firebell went at two o'clock in the morning, and the telephone instantly became the town's worried nerve. Whose house was it? This was one of the few times when I felt like a professional newspaperman. I rang the exchange, and Fred Gibson told me it was the MacGibbons' house on Moon Street.

'I can see her from here, Kit,' he shouted. 'She's a beaut . . .'

The big bell in the fire station was still clanging. Our whole household was up, and Tom was already dressed and snarling at me because two days ago I had stripped a tyre off his bike for my own, since my needs were always professional.

'Hurry up,' he shouted impatiently from the back door. 'You'll have to dink me.'

I dressed over my pyjamas: a pair of trousers, jacket, shoes without socks, but Tom was properly dressed. Like my father he would sooner be lopped off like a dead flower than look carelessly dressed.

'I thought you didn't like to watch fires,' I taunted him.

'I don't,' he said irritably as he sat on the cross-bar of the bike, 'but what can I do? I've *got* to see it, that's all.'

With his left foot on the pedal to help me we wavered blindly through the dark town, but when we entered Moon Street we could see the flames. A crowd of townspeople and neighbours were in the street watching the MacGibbon house burn. A fair-sized pile of MacGibbon clothes, kitchen equipment and furniture was out on the roadway, the local firemen were working very efficiently against a superior force, and the MacGibbons (save Lockie himself who was out of town) were standing with their belongings, dressed in overcoats over nightclothes – Mrs MacGibbon and two daughters. The youngest, who was nicknamed Smilie, was weeping, but the other one was taking it very well, which was not unusual for the MacGibbons because they had to be a family of living philosophers to face the regular disasters that Lockie's speculative existence often brought them to.

I leaned against the bike and watched the flames burning down the front bedroom. Two dolls on the mantelpiece burned like religious idols, and the springs of a stuffed armchair suddenly burst through the burning cloth and we heard the twang. Some of the furniture was still untouched even in the flaming heart of this private little hell, but nobody made any attempt to rescue anything now.

'We could get some of it out,' Tom said nervously.

Nobody paid any attention to him.

He shifted on his feet and we watched a piano go. For Tom to be rendered helpless like this was an affront to his blossoming manhood, so he suddenly jumped over the hoses and ran up the path and disappeared into the side of the house where the flames were not so hot. He emerged like a frightened pigeon dragging something behind him. It was an ironing board. Its cloth surface was on fire so he beat out the flames fiercely as he ran back and dumped it in the street near Mrs MacGibbon, his face red and his blond hair scorched.

'Jesus Christ, Tom,' Mrs MacGibbon said incredulously to him. 'What did you do that for?'

Tom didn't hear.

'You're crazy,' I shouted at him. 'You're just showing off.'

'You don't even understand,' he said angrily and then walked away in disgust.

But I understood. Tom was just beginning to feel all the frustrations which life had arranged for a man rather than a boy. Everything, in fact, was bigger and more powerful than he had imagined, so one blow (any blow) at the monstrous opposition was better than standing by and doing nothing.

*

The MacGibbon fire was something to talk about for a day or two and when Lockie came back from the neighbouring town of Nooah, where he had been organizing a boxing championship among the fruit pickers, he was given a lot of sympathy because he was well liked. The family moved into an old house by the river and being a Catholic the church helped Lockie to get a few things together, although miraculously they had rescued a fair quantity of their belongings.

But in a few weeks it was all forgotten, although fire – the Stoic future – had somehow entered our family life. Tom had a row with my father about his visits to an old locomotive fitter living in one of the railway houses. He was an old German named Hans Dreiser and he was giving Tom Left Book Club books on the Spanish War to read. My father threw one of them onto the kitchen fire, and Tom threatened to retaliate by burning a copy of Walter Pater's *Renaissance* which he would obviously never do because Tom had an intellectual respect for the printed book which was almost religious. He wouldn't even have burned *Mein Kampf*.

About two weeks after the MacGibbon fire Mr Dorman Walker, the local representative for the Australian Univermag Fire Insurance Company and also a local grain and feed merchant, came to my father, who was the local legal adviser to the insurance company, and said that Lockie MacGibbon was demanding £500 insurance due on his house. Dorman Walker was convinced that Lockie had deliberately burned down his house to collect the insurance which was perfectly in character, but my father didn't believe it. Despite his moral Pygmalionism he never thought the legal worst of anyone, and he wasn't going to suspect Lockie on the word of Dorman Walker who was a wizened and dried-up little man. He also had the lawyer's instinctive doubt about conviction instead of fact.

Yet he knew it was a possibility he would have to look into. At first he told Walker that the police should be informed and that they should investigate if there was any suggestion of criminal conspiracy to defraud, but Dorman Walker (he was an Australian Protestant but my father despised him for his lack of pride and his tricking methods) pointed out that the local police were all Lockie's friends, and the Chief Constable Sergeant Joe Collins, was a Catholic, so nobody in the police station was going to investigate Lockie's house burning down, any more than they investigated Lockie's illegal two-up schools across the river on the New South Wales side every Sunday morning. Walker also happened to know that, as usual, Lockie was in money trouble; but this time he had two heavy debts due which amounted to £1,000 and he was on the verge of bankruptcy.

'All right,' my father said to Walker. 'I'll send Tom with you to look at the house. But no underhand trickery or spying, Walker,' my father ordered. 'Everything out in the open.'

We all hated spying, in fact we were brought up to believe that openness and honour were brothers, and in this Tom was the model pupil, even though he was beginning to treat the rest of the family morality with rich contempt.

Tom went next day with Walker to inspect the house – a legal privilege the insurance agent had a right to, but which Lockie naturally resented although he could not refuse permission. Tom probably liked playing detective, although I think he liked the legal game better because like my father he believed profoundly in the deep internal rightness of the law, and he considered it a birthright which he was not going to betray for anyone, no matter what old Hans Dreiser taught him.

Had Lockie MacGibbon really burned down his house for the insurance money?

For the same reason that my father sent Tom, Lockie MacGibbon sent his elder daughter Margaret (she had two or three other names as well, but we naturally called her Peggy) to see that there was no funny business. Up till then, even on the night of the fire, I doubt if Tom and Peggy had exchanged more than a hundred sentences all their lives, and now that they were meeting under difficult circumstances there was bound to be trouble. Lockie, professionally, was inclined to be devious as well as bold; he had to be; but his wife and daughters were rather full-figured, reddish-brown and golden women who were daunted by nothing.

Peggy was seventeen, on the eve of eighteen, and she had red hair and green gay eyes and was further along into womanhood than Tom was into manhood, although Tom was the same age. She resembled her attractive mother, and she had a reputation for taunting and tempting the boys. It was really her green gay eyes that did it. Peggy's eyes were the main nerve of her lovely body and her cheeky

mind; they met and asked curious little questions of everyone in town. That was probably what began to make her
attractive to men, because she seemed to inspect you very
boldly and think about you and ask provocative questions
about you and maybe offer you something, so that men
usually made the mistake of seeing in her teasing curi-
osity an attractive invitation. But I guessed what it really
was, although I don't think even Peggy herself knew what
gave her this undeserved reputation.

Peggy was, in fact, a very moral girl because she believed in her religion and was afraid of the Fathers; and
in a Catholic household of two girls the chances were that
one of them would have to go to Castlemaine to become a
nun, and it might very well be Peggy. Or, like her mother
who had once been on the musical comedy stage, Peggy
might become a dancer (she was already one of our cham-
pion Highland dancers). Either way seemed a perfect possibility for her. But I must admit it was hard to imagine her
a nun because she had a streak of daring in her, and like her
father she was a mocker, and she taunted Tom unmercifully
as he dug around in the ashes under the massive piles of
twisted corrugated iron.

'You're just like two rats poking around a rubbish tip,'
she said contemptuously to Tom and Dorman Walker.
'Rats!'

Tom blushed.

Every time they looked at the charred bones of some
burnt-out piece of MacGibbon furniture, Peggy would say
haughtily to them: 'Don't touch that! You've no right.' And
when Tom inspected the tin bathtub which was lying on
its side she said furiously to him: 'Leave that alone. You
ought to be ashamed.'

'Listen, Peggy,' Tom said. 'We're only trying to find out
where the fire started.'

'What for? You've no right.'

'Yes we have. What about the insurance?'

'You're mad!' Peggy told him. 'Do you think Lockie would have left any trace if he'd set the house on fire?'

'But we're just trying to find out where it started,' Tom insisted again.

'It started in the roof,' Peggy told him. 'Spontaneous combustion,' she mocked.

Tom was too serious and too legally preoccupied to match that sort of ridicule, so he blushed again and began stubbornly to dig deeper. The more Peggy mocked him with her green eyes that day, the more he rummaged in that black ash heap for evidence of Lockie's guilt.

'You're not going to find anything,' Peggy said after an hour when she was getting fed up. 'You don't even know where to look.'

'Don't worry,' Tom said ominously. 'I've found something already.'

'What?'

'If you've found something,' Dorman Walker interrupted sharply, 'keep it to yourself, Tom. Don't give away evidence.'

Dorman Walker always looked shrivelled up, and he was sitting miserably hot under a peppercorn tree, sunk in the shade. It was noon by now and they were all smeared and black with dusty ash.

'You're a pig,' Peggy said to Dorman Walker. 'And if you're so smart,' she added to Tom, 'why do you have to work for your silly father?'

Tom dug stubbornly for another five minutes to counter this insult.

'Dirty bloody twisters!' Peggy said furiously and suddenly left them.

There was nothing new in this situation. We were so

used to such off-hand taunts in the town that we had adapted ourselves to them in different ways. Being twenty, and born an Australian, I had long given in to this Australian sport, because I was fed up with the contest and willingly accepted defeat. My fifteen-year-old sister, Jean, had a hot temper, but her expensive school kept her above it all. Only Tom was not so well equipped, because he was too seriously handicapped by his hot conscience. He was more like my father than any of us, yet he was already beginning to be bitterly contemptuous of the status-quo which all our morality was concerned with, whether Australian or English, because he was beginning to see it from a different point of view. I suppose Tom's changing attitude was mainly the work of old Hans Dreiser, the red railwayman, or rather it was the result of the time we lived in – our futureless future, the hypocrisies of our politicians and our priests, and the corruption of an outside world in which the Japanese were then ravaging Manchuria, the Italians had used gas in Abyssinia, and Guernica had been destroyed by German bombers, while Mr Eden insisted nobly on non-intervention.

Once, when I had asked Tom what he saw in old Dreiser, and his politics, Tom replied with untarnished naïveté: 'He wants to save the world.'

'How?' I asked drily. 'With all those books of his?'

'I don't know, Kit, but that's what I want to do myself.'

'What?'

'Save the whole bloody world.'

I laughed, but Tom meant it almost breathlessly, and when Peggy MacGibbon brought her normal Australian (not Catholic) sporting instinct to ridicule this world-saver, Tom's only defence was to become stubbornly more serious and therefore more vulnerable. The next time she passed Tom in the street Peggy sang a few words of a Calvinist hymn at him: '*Work for the night is coming* ...' The rest of the hymn, in the Catholic version, was a very vulgar joke about the Calvinist honesty in daylight and the dirty Calvinist trickery in darkness.

It was a good parody, but Tom was indignant because we were not Calvinists, and he was not darkly dishonest. He could think of nothing to say in reply, so he tried to ignore her, but Peggy's laughter followed him down the street.

It was really unfortunate that they had both become so involved in a silly adult quarrel, because they were only being used, both of them, by my father and Lockie as a sort of probing skirmish for what was obviously going to be an open battle between the two sides if it really were true that Lockie had set fire to his own house. In fact an open war between the two of them had been inevitable for some time, probably since the day two years before when Lockie had designed and built a float which he displayed in the local hospital fête procession depicting my father, barely disguised, as a stuffed Puritan with six arms: one holding a Bible, the second a crown, the third a hangman's noose, the fourth a bag of gold, the fifth a petticoat and the sixth a top hat. This was just after my father had represented the Sunday Observance Society in a court action against 'Touchy' Green, a friend of Lockie's who had tried to open his skating rink as a Club on Sundays. It was a good but inaccurate joke, an unfair attack in my father's opinion, not only because he had simply been doing his lawyer's job (even if he relished it) but because there was no way of effectively replying to it except to sue Lockie for defamation, which my father was intelligent enough not to do, though barely. He called the Hospital chairman a blackguard for permitting it and never spoke to him again and even refused to defend the hospital in a suit brought by a farmer who claimed (correctly) to have had his leg amputated without good cause.

But if it hadn't been that particular incident, it would have been something else on either side because he and Lockie had both been working up to an open clash, and this time it looked as if some sort of final battle was on the way, because Tom was also convinced, after his inspection of the ashes, that Lockie had set fire to his own house. This meant it would probably end in court, in which case I knew that I would not like to be Lockie MacGibbon.

5

Tom, in fact, had found nothing at all. But Dorman Walker told my father that the fire had started in the tin bathtub which, he said, had been half-filled with petrol and set on fire through the waste pipe which had acted as a sort of fuse from the garden (there was no sewage system).

'Ridiculous,' my father said.

'I'll stand by that, no matter what you say,' Walker argued.

'Tom. You agree with that nonsensical theory?'

'Something like that happened,' Tom said reluctantly. 'There had been petrol or something like it in that bath.'

'Can you prove it?'

'How can I prove it?' Dorman Walker said angrily.

'Then don't bother me with it until you can,' my father told him. For a moment it looked as if Dorman Walker was going to say something defiant to my father, but he quailed at the last moment under that contemptuous and commanding English eye.

The next morning when we were eating breakfast Lockie MacGibbon hammered at our back door and shouted out: 'Quayle! Come on out here, you pommie bastard, I want to talk to you.'

We all heard it from the breakfast room, and my father leapt up, threw his napkin on the table and opened the kitchen door and said to Lockie: 'Get out. Get off my property. Do you think you can come in here using language like that . . .' He was exploding.

'Oh, calm down,' Lockie said cheerfully. 'A little more dirty language and a lot less dirty legal trickery would be a bloody sight better coming from you, Qualie. Where's my bathtub?'

'What bathtub?'

'You sent Tom or some dirty bastard to steal that bathtub from the ashes of my house, so where is it?'

'I did no such thing,' my father shouted, 'so get out of here or I'll take a whip to you.'

'Hah!' Lockie mocked. He was no bigger than my father, and face-to-face they looked like bantam-cocks scratching at the dust in preparation for a fight to the death. 'I want that bathtub back,' Lockie said. 'That's stealing. I'm going down to Joe Collins (the police) if you don't have it back by tonight.'

'Go to Collins,' my father roared. 'I'll go myself if you don't.'

'What a dirty bastard,' Lockie said off-handedly as he turned to go.

'If you use that word again I'll crack you,' my father roared.

'Silly bastard!' Lockie said as a parting shot, and my father, who loved violent words but detested violence itself, stood frustratingly still as Lockie slammed the gate and laughed as he got into his silver Marmon and soared off.

The rest of us had been listening, fascinated. My mother was a gentle and good-natured Manxwoman who was perpetually trying to make both ends meet and who was just entering the age in late middle life when she wondered too often whether she would ever see Ethan Vannen again, but she had the Gaelic humour and so did I and so did Jean. We all thought it very funny, but Tom didn't. We rather admired Lockie's cheeky and irrepressible attack. But Tom was the kind who, in some future House of Parliament, would be an opponent not only on the floor of the Chamber but outside in the corridors as well. A war was a war.

In fact my father also burst out laughing when he came in, and he said – offering it up to heaven as a private joke: 'Bathtub! Where's my bathtub . . .'

We all knew where the bathtub was. Obviously Dorman Walker had sneakingly stolen it in the night to have it chemically analysed for evidence, and though I had expected my father to storm in and ring up Walker and demand an explanation of such underhand behaviour, he just went on laughing and repeating upwards: 'Where's my bathtub. . . .'

'Nonetheless,' Tom said. 'That was a dirty trick of Dorman Walker's. He must have taken it away last night.'

'It serves MacGibbon right,' my father said firmly.

But Tom, in his present moral condition, felt responsible.

*

Perhaps I should point out once again that Tom was then of an age when everything he did mattered. He was almost eighteen and everything elated him or everything hurt; everything good and bad simply crowded in on his heart. He had even given up dancing (which he was good at) because it was partly a deception, yet physically life was still a huge joy in him which was trying desperately to get out, only he could not find enough explosive exits for it, except the hunting and swimming he did.

The youth of our town were all good swimmers, because we all worshipped the low summer river as a ritual release from the inactivity of winter. In winter the Murray was high and fast and mean and untouchable, but in summer it was low and clear and generous. In winter we had paddle steamers and floods, and in summer we fished and swam, and like Tom Sawyer and Huck Finn we lived for all that the river could give us. Tom was one of the best swimmers in the town, and because it was a hot summer and because the days dragged out lazily in listless dust and sleepy noondays, we would all go down to the Murray on Saturdays to swim in a big hole which had a small island about eight feet by five feet in it. We called it Dog Island because it had once been shaped like a dog's head.

Each summer when the river was low and the island was visible the annual sport on Dog Island was to remain on it if you could. To stand up on it was an invitation to be pushed off it, and with a little water splashed on its surface it became so slippery that it was impossible to stand up even if someone pushed you lightly. Tom still liked this physical nonsense, probably because it was a sporting substitute for his fighting days. We had some gay and tough fights on that island. Tom was strong and wiry, a determined and unquenchable opponent for any challenger, but often he would tumble off in the middle of a contest simply because he had dissolved helplessly in laughter.

On this particular day a schism had appeared in the mixture of youths in the swimming hole. An eighteen-year-old pugilist named Finn MacCooil, an admirer and supporter of Lockie MacGibbon, announced that he and his mates would make sure that no more Quayles were ever going to get on Dog Island again. Finn was a wild Australian boy who had been shaping up to somebody since the age of four. His father had been a river-boat captain who had wrecked his boat on the Swan Rapids a mile from town and thereafter had become one of the town drunkards. Finn had no mother and was brought up recklessly by nobody, or by neighbours, and sometimes by the sympathetic nuns, and the result was a tough, amoral mess. He was recklessly loose with the girls and I had already seen Finn drunk in the gutter on Saturday nights. Finn thought of himself as Lockie's bodyguard and henchman, in gratitude perhaps for Lockie's efforts to build him up as a local prizefighter. As a fighter (lightweight) Finn was a natural executioner, anything he didn't like he would go 'ssss' to, as if he intended to crush it, and whenever he was fighting in the ring (in one of Lockie's promoted contests) he would announce all his best hooks and jabs with this little 'ssss' and he could not break himself of the habit, so it reduced his chances of going very far in the ring.

Finn and Tom were very much alike in some ways, but they were also opposites and they knew it and disliked each other, and though Finn's Australian pride was large in his stocky stringy body, he and Tom had never fought as boys, although how they had missed doing so I don't know. I think they were both afraid of each other, or afraid of the result. Now it was getting a bit late for serious violence between them, so sporting violence was the next best thing and with a few other youths – Jack Dobey (whom we called Dobey the Diver) and Peter MacGilray and Ford Johnson, all Catholics but not yet enemies, Finn MacCooil was issuing a challenge. Tom gladly accepted it and got onto the island and threw two of them off, one of them Finn himself, and I threw the third and fourth off and we waited for them to return.

The inevitable happened. We had our friends, they had theirs. Tom's friends were the Philby twins (who were the drover's sons) and Fred Dreiser, old Dreiser's nephew, and I also had my friends, so it became a violent battle between us and them, involving fifteen or twenty youths and no holds barred: an edgily friendly-unfriendly contest. It only ended when, in a tangle of arms and legs that looked like a thousand interlocked worms tied in a huge knot, we all went over together. But Tom, on the fringe of the mess, came down heavily on Peggy MacGibbon's shoulder and they sank together. Peggy had been standing nearby barracking her family supporters.

Tom didn't know immediately who it was but he knew he had hit someone very heavily, and even while under water he was pulling her up. She was a good swimmer but she was dazed and Tom helped her up onto the slippery little island and we all got up and crowded around Peggy who was lying on her back. Tom was bending over her and brushing her long wet red hair from her freckled face, and I could see how he looked and how she looked. Her dazed eyes gradually focused and they focused on Tom. And Tom, worried and upset, exchanged the panic in his heart for the surprised look she gave him and I knew that in his concern and in her sudden view of Tom as a gentle and honest boy as well as a morally tough one, or of something else that was in him that I didn't see, they had met each other in another way.

'Are you all right?' he said.

'Yes,' she said quickly and sat up. 'Just let me get up.'

The moment was gone. It was replaced with another: accusations from the Lockie faction that Tom had deliberately attacked a woman. Tom pushed three of them off Dog Island in one go, furious. Finn was the first to go because Tom blamed him for everything that had happened. But the rest threw him in and then jumped off and swam away with Peggy, who had turned her back on the fracas and called them to come away. The Catholic boys stood on the other side of the river and led by Finn MacCooil sang to us their insulting version of 'Work for the night is coming . . .' We sang in answer 'Oh where, oh where has Lockie's bathtub gone? Oh where, oh where can it be?'

*

It was primitive fun, but its results were not so primitive because one of Lockie's supporters, Dobey the Diver, had broken his right wrist. Dobey was a likeable and quiet and shipwrecked boy who had once been clever, had matriculated brilliantly, had tried to get work for his clever head, had tried to become a bank clerk, but he was the milkman's son so nobody would look at him as anything but a labourer, even though he had passed the bank's entrance exam with excellent results. Of all the boys on Dog Island that day Dobey the Diver and I were the only ones with real jobs, although both were temporary. Dobey was now a temporary weigher-and-packer at the butter factory. He was also twenty and he could dive ninety-five feet off the top of the town bridge into the river below, something nobody else could do, which is why we called him Dobey the Diver. But unlucky Dobey, with a broken wrist, could no longer weigh and pack butter so he was suddenly out of work.

Peggy also suffered unpleasant side effects from that fight. She had swallowed a great deal of muddy water and she was ill in bed for several days, and Tom was noticeably preoccupied and jumpy during that time.

A year before this I had been suddenly and violently in love myself with a country girl named Jennifer Owen with whom I never exchanged a word, so I guessed what was happening to Tom. I was not surprised when my sister reported that he had been seen one night sitting like a little tiger under a gum tree opposite the house by the river where the MacGibbons lived, staring at it in what was probably a puzzled condition. Like Demeter waiting longingly at the gates of Hell for Persephone to appear, Tom now wanted to see the Peggy MacGibbon he had never seen at all until a few days ago. The old Peggy had disappeared into the earth, now a new one would surely appear.

I wondered if Peggy was lying in bed hypnotized like Tom

by that same snap of the gods' fingers. Much later Peggy told me that she lay in bed staring at the cloud-like stains on the filthy ceiling of that old wooden house and seeing nothing but the unfinished face and the melting blue eyes and stubborn mouth of what was obviously going to be a wonderful man – Tom Quayle.

A week passed and they still did not see each other again, although I saw Peggy one day when I was at the railway station reporting the arrival of the examiners and judges for the three-day singing contests which were a big event in the district. Peggy was at the station to meet Mrs Craig Campbell who taught Highland Dancing which would be part of another competition during the Agricultural Show in three weeks' time. Peggy was one of the contestants.

'Are you all right, Peg?' I asked her casually as we passed.

She looked at me accusingly as if I had suddenly startled her. I was his brother so I suppose even I meant something different. 'Of course I'm all right,' she said indignantly and hurried away.

They now longed to meet each other, but under what circumstances? Every Saturday night in St Helen all the shops in the main street and the six pubs remained open until 9 p.m. and everybody came to the main street (Dunlap Street) to see friends, show off their best clothes, eat pie and peas and ice-cream in the cafés, buy a week's provisions (if you came from the country) and parade up and down the well-lit half-mile of low, verandahed shops. Cars, buggies and horses lined the roadway under the pepper trees and gum trees, and tempting groups of young men teased tempting groups of young women, and a sharp, concentrated sort of love-making was promised in the quick eyes of those Saturday nights. Sometimes it matured and sometimes it did not, but some Saturday nights, particularly in summer, the street was electric with silent, adolescent promises from one sex to the other.

Naturally Peggy, with her red hair and dancing feet and cheeky eyes, was a lively part of this love parade. She walked up and down Dunlap Street with Smilie her sister on that particular Saturday night looking for Tom, anxious to exchange one more message from green eyes to blue, from blue eyes to green – just to see what was really there. But Tom had already given up the peacocking of Saturday nights on Dunlap Street, and lately he had been going instead to old Dreiser's house by the railway line where the old German was teaching him the moral right and moral wrong of the condition of the world.

There was something stronger here than Peggy's green eyes. Tom was already a good pupil for Hans Dreiser's dialectics because he had learned his lesson in moral responsibility from my father. Despite its bigotry, my father's eccentric morality was also a form of social obligation. Morals, he had always taught us in his dogmatic way, are a matter of self-realization for the attainment of good; legal obligation required coercion – but moral obligation must stem from inner compulsion. But though he even went so far as to accept the Socratic idea that no man is willingly vicious and that all vice is ignorance, he insisted that moral law could *never* be the true nature of man, it could only be the will of God. He had, in fact, constructed his entire life on this contradictory mélange of rational moral law and a blind man's religion, and he had tried to hand it on to us almost by force.

That was where it all fell down for Tom (I didn't care either way) because no God could answer the problems old Dreiser was now putting on his conscience. In action my father's morality reduced itself to the pettiest and most obvious rules for behaviour: going to church was right whereas swearing was wrong, paying your bills was right and gambling was wrong, respectability was right and drunkenness was wrong, and above all the unquestioning attitude to things as they were was right (God, King, Country and the Rule of the Law), whereas questioning the existing structure of our lives was wrong. He had two simple codes for all this : the Bible and the Statute Book.

But Tom was already dissatisfied with both, although he read and puzzled over the English Statutes, the Court of Appeal Decisions and the twenty-seven volumes of Mews' Case Law all day in his cubby hole in my father's office. But there were no moral or civil laws that could solve our problems. Like Tom, we were all being consumed by something more powerful than God, and dictated to by social laws outside any written constitution. Every workless boy now getting drunk on Saturday night in Dunlap Street knew in his soul that he was already a goner. He knew he was being brutally cheated, that he was wasting every valuable hour of his valuable youth simply because there was nothing useful to do with it. Could we construct, invent, or move the mountains of slag that poured wastefully into our souls? For someone like Tom, trying to construct his own moral obligation to the world, there was far too much injustice and misery and waste to be happily drunk on Dunlap Street. He was on fire, and old Dreiser was feeding the flames with the practical but dreamlike answers my father never did have. The old German offered to reconstruct the whole world by exposing the rot, and by removing ignorance and class and exploitation. He was offering to replace these evils with usefulness, invention, opportunity and some form of social collective which would clean up the mess we lived in.

So Tom was not on Dunlap Street looking for Peggy MacGibbon's green eyes, not yet anyway, he was down at the old man's house sitting under the big red gums looking

39

out over the moonlit river, listening to the million frogs on the Billabong while Dreiser recited Goethe, Lessing and Shelley to him on the morality of action.

And on that Saturday Tom was inspired enough to want to act. It was not an easy thing that he did, not at all as easy as it seems now. The next day being Sunday Tom announced at breakfast that he was not going to Church.

'Oh? Aren't you?' my father said, poised on a wing, ready to attack. 'Why not may I ask?'

'How conceive a God supremely good,' Tom said, 'who heaps his favours on the sons he loves, yet scatters evil with as large a hand ...'

'What's *that*?'

Tom dug himself into his chair to stick it out because here was real blasphemy. 'Voltaire.' he said.

'Leave the breakfast table this minute,' my father shouted in astonishment. 'Do you intend to question God in your own house? On Sunday?' he roared, getting up and standing over Tom who had not moved. 'You bring that sort of language from that foul German into this house.'

'I'm not going to Church,' Tom said, his stubborn face set tight.

I was amazed at his courage, and my father was so incensed that he was about to box Tom's ears, but my mother suddenly intervened. 'Oh, for heaven's sake let him think it out for himself,' she said to my father. 'Let him alone, Edward Quayle.' My mother's way of reprimanding my father was always to turn him into some stranger called Edward Quayle.

'Think for himself!' my father groaned. 'What sort of thinking is this?'

It raged on, but Tom sat still and stuck it out. My father threatened and appealed to Heaven for judgement, but he must have known already that Tom was on the way out, he was on the way to some other kind of solution, some other kind of morality, and dogmatic argument would not help. Tom won his point – with my mother's help, and when he got up from the table that day he went outside and got his rifle and went across the river to the Billabong to hunt rabbit and fox, which was his only means of getting cash. He said savagely that this being his first challenge to that mad God they all talked about, he was going to make it pay.

It seemed simple enough, but I knew it had been much more painful than that. Six months before, coming home late and passing the verandah where Tom now slept summer and winter, the way I had done, I had heard him praying desperately and resentfully to my father's God: 'Don't desert me, for Christ's sake. Don't just go out on me. At least don't let me stop believing . . .'

He was almost accusing God of desertion, but he was also begging grimly for help against Voltaire. Help had not arrived, because he had now come to this open break. My father would go on objecting angrily, but my mother would defend Tom, even in his blundering agnosticism, because Tom's soft blue eyes always attracted some instinctive desire in all women to look after him in a fight. Not only my mother would look after him, but my sister Jeannie would always guard his flank in a family argument, even against my father to whom she was very attached. I supposed that Peggy had now fallen for those guileless orbs. I think their deep, childlike honesty made women feel safe with him; they knew he would never betray them. Fortunately Tom knew nothing of this and would have denied his attractions vehemently.

My mother also trusted Tom's judgement of himself, and so did I. I sympathized with his rebellion, but I did nothing to help him. Though twenty, I still went to church because I did not want to fight my father, I did not want to crash my head against those stubborn Victorian walls the way Tom did.

One thing did occur to me though. Lockie MacGibbon, like my father, thought old Dreiser a terrible menace to the safety of all decent people. If asked to propose a common enemy, Lockie and Edward J. Quayle would have picked the old German, which now gave Tom a problem, because Peggy would agree with them. Peggy was a good girl in her religion and would never abandon it for Tom's Protestantism; even less for his latest denial of a Heavenly Father.

6

My father began believing in Lockie's guilt when someone (we knew it was Finn MacCooil) broke into Dorman Walker's feed and grain barn. Finn and his friends had turned the place upside down, obviously looking for the tin bathtub. Not finding anything they had ripped open dozens of bags of chaff and poured liquid fertilizer all over the granary floor. Dorman Walker's wizened little face mixed tears of rage in his tea-coloured sweat, and my English father was shocked at such wantonness, and he was determined thereafter to pursue Lockie MacGibbon to the very jaws of justice, though once more it fell to Tom to do the dirty work.

In the meantime Tom and Peggy did meet again, though under peculiar and not happy circumstances. Every summer in St Helen two or three people would be drowned in the Murray River, either because they were careless or because the river, in certain parts, was far more dangerous than its wide, slow, summer surface suggested. Like a house burning down, these drowning tragedies touched everybody because we usually knew the victim well.

This time it was a garage owner named Fyfe Angus who had driven his two daughters (12 and 9) up the river three or four miles to a famous fishing spot called Burke's Crossing where the old explorer was supposed to have crossed the river. Fyfe had been walking across some rapids in a shallow but swift bend in the river looking for mussels when he had

43

literally disappeared. Kathy, the eldest girl, had run across the snake-infested and swampy Billabong to the nearest house which belonged to a Greek peach farmer named Goliath. He had telephoned the town and broken the news in his few words of frightened English. Everybody who could get away rushed by car out to Burke's Crossing. Fyfe Angus was drowned, but his body had to be recovered and some of the best young swimmers of the town went out to help. Tom came out with me on the back of the Philby twins' motor-cycle combination.

There were already seven or eight cars on the river bank when we arrived and six people were diving in the very deep hole just beyond the rapids. It was full of snags and tricky downward currents which could carry a swimmer under the huge rotting trees sunk in the hole. In parts you could not reach bottom, and that was obviously where Fyfe now lay. Someone had taken his younger daughter home, but the older one, Kathy, was sitting on the mud-bank watching the scene with dry childish eyes. She refused to go away so some of the women sat near her. Her mother was at her sister's place 200 miles away and had been sent for. Lockie MacGibbon arrived in his Marmon and Peggy was with him.

We all stood around watching the town boys dive in the hole, and one by one they became exhausted by the current and someone else took their place. It was already getting dark, and by the time Tom went in for his spell they had switched on the headlights of some of the cars to light up the hole, and I watched Tom in the shadows lift his head, drop it, lift his backside and his legs and go straight down. They were all after the bottom now, but nobody (including Finn MacCooil and Dobey the Diver) could reach it.

I watched Tom closely, a little worried, because I knew how he hated to be defeated by distance, depth or the mocking power of the unattainable; and so did Peggy watch him. Lockie had thoughtfully brought some whisky for the divers, and he handed it around and Peggy sat near Kathy Angus and watched Tom come up, go down, come up, go down. After an hour I could see that Tom was getting very tired, because he was now being carried too far downstream by the fast currents, so I shouted at him to come out and after a couple more dives he swam to the slippery edge of the bank and crawled up a few yards and just lay there, exhausted and cold.

Somebody flung a towel over him. He turned his face a little and saw that it was Peggy, who sat down near him and didn't say anything. They knew their own feelings meant nothing here, and that probably helped them.

But when Tom tried to get up she pushed him firmly down again with a quick proprietary air. It was dark and nobody could see them. Then Peggy produced a bottle of Lockie's whisky, which was a nicely normal thing in Lockie's house where drinking whisky was not evil.

She handed Tom the bottle. I knew he had never touched a drop of spirits in his life, not because it was immoral but because he had looked at what was happening to his old schoolmates on Saturday nights and knew it was too stupid to copy. I wondered whether he would have taken that bottle from any other hand, because he sat up, took it, poured a good mouthful of the whisky down his throat, swallowed some and spat the rest out.

'My God. How do they drink that stuff?' he said.

Peggy did not laugh. She said with matriarchal intensity: 'Drink it! *Don't* spit it out.'

Tom drank again and pulled a face and swallowed a good dose and returned the bottle. Then he fell back again, and Tom the animal went to sleep. Peggy went on sitting there for a while until her father called her in the darkness and she got up and went over to the Marmon, but she came back again and said to Tom when he woke up: 'You ought to get dressed. You'll get your death of cold.'

'No,' he said. 'I'm going in again.'

'You're mad!' she told him calmly and walked off.

Tom told me then that he had been thinking. Most of his breath was wasted, he said, using energy to get down to any depth. He was sure that if he took a big stone and simply held his breath and let it take him down, it might be slower but he would certainly go deeper, because he would use up less air and energy. He wanted me to help him get a big stone into the water. The only trouble was that there were no stones, so over the protests of the Philby boys he borrowed their tool-bag from the motor-bike and a piece of canvas, and he wrapped one of the big dried mud-cakes in the canvas, attached the tools to it, tied it all to a piece of very long rope and together we staggered across the rapids, holding the weight between us. He got into the water and he shouted above the swishing noise of the rapids: 'Give me the short end of the rope, Kit, and keep the long end yourself. Then throw in the sack when I say Go.' I gave him the short end of the rope and he wrapped it around his fist and said: 'Let her go!' I dropped the lump into the hole and as Tom went down with it I played out the rope. The signal for ascent was two sharp tugs. By now there was only one man diving beside Tom, the rest had given up, so everybody watched what was happening, and we waited.

He was a very long time under water and I was getting ready to pull him up without his signal when he suddenly tugged and I pulled him up. He exploded to the surface blowing out a huge breath.

'I was on the bottom,' he announced.

'Where are my tools?' Tod Philby shouted.

I pulled up the end of the rope and the tools and the canvas sack were on it, but most of the mud-cake had dissolved. We got another big square of dried mud and tied it up in the canvas and prepared to repeat the performance, and everybody was poised now as Tom wrapped the short end of the rope around his fist.

'Okay,' he said and I threw in the heavy sack.

Tom was pulled down after it, and I let the long rope slip through my fingers. I have never forgotten that long silent wait under the black and yellow glare of the lamps on that pool of otherwise pleasant water. It would never be the same again for any of us; we had always enjoyed it before but now it was a death hole. I thought about it even as I waited, and we waited a very long time and I heard Peggy shout from the bank: 'Pull him up, Kit. He must be caught on something.'

But I could feel him on the end of the rope and since we had agreed again that I should not pull him up unless he gave me two sharp tugs I did not interfere. I think Tom must have been under water well over a minute and a half because everybody was shouting at me 'Pull him up, pull him up!' particularly Peggy who had run out along the rapids towards me and was screaming in my ear.

But I knew Tom better than they did, and I had, like my mother, a profound confidence in his ability to survive on his own terms so I did not pull. I waited for his signal and when it came I began to pull. This time it was a dead weight and even before I had taken in a quarter of the rope Tom himself emerged, and I knew that I had Fyfe Angus on the bottom of the long end of this haul.

Tom was bleeding from the nose, and his face was covered in blood, but my burden was too important to bother with Tom. Everybody watched and some of them helped except Peggy who, hiding behind everybody else's preoccupation, pulled Tom out and he stood on the edge breathing heavily while Peggy gave him a towel. With half an ear I heard her saying to him anxiously:

'Look at you. Why are you bleeding?'

'I don't know, Peg,' Tom said, wiping his hands as if trying to wipe the death off them. 'I'm all right. I don't feel anything.'

'You'll have to go to a doctor. It's awful . . .'

'I'm all right . . .'

'But you're not! There's blood all over you.'

'It's just my nose.'

'Why are you being so stubborn. You might even be hurt internally.'

Tom said he didn't think so. In any case Fyfe was now on the surface and we could see tangled into his muddy shirt a branch of a black tree. He must have fallen in, tangled with one of the rotting trunks which caught his shirt, struggled to free himself and drowned. In this struggle he probably broke off the rotting branch, but too late, and he sank to the bottom of the hole.

The rest of it is not important here. The tragedy was over, or rather the tragedy was completed by that blown limp remnant of our local garage owner. Tom's nose had stopped bleeding and we assumed it was pressure bursting a tiny vessel somewhere in his sinuses. We had no intention of spending money on a doctor to find out.

That wasn't the problem for Tom anyway. His problem now was how and where and when to see Peggy openly. They were both too proud to hide their heads about it: they did not want to see each other secretly. Yet both knew that if they met anywhere publicly the novelty and the irony of the situation would soon hot up the whole town's gossipy nerves. Everybody knew of the antagonism between Lockie and my father, and everybody knew that it was now developing into an open conflict over Lockie's insurance.

But neither Tom nor Peggy could flaunt themselves in the face of their families, so they decided nothing and promised nothing and asked nothing of each other, as if leaving it to a generous God to solve their problems for them. But since there are no generous gods their problem only became more complicated, because my father sent Tom quietly to the neighbouring town of Nooah to find out if Lockie had really stayed there on the night his house burned down, or whether he had secretly returned in his silver Marmon and fired the house himself.

7

By Friday of that week, Tom, playing detective, discovered that Lockie had very good friends and alibis in Nooah, but there were other people who swore that Lockie's Marmon had been heard zooming along the country road towards St Helen that disastrous night. Nobody travelled our roads much in the middle of the night, and in those days all cars were distinctive in sound as well as appearance, and Lockie MacGibbon's 'streaky bullet' was easily identifiable from a half-mile away, unseen.

'The Curries heard him, the Stones and Mrs Mills said he woke up their dogs and they barked for hours,' Tom told my father over dinner.

'Did anybody actually see him?' my father asked.

'Judo Wallace saw him.' Judo was a canal inspector. It was not unusual in summer for Judo to be out at night in the country opening lock gates for the irrigation canals that came off the river higher up and often ran at night to avoid evaporation.

'Did you get Wallace's affidavit?'

'Not a chance,' Tom said. 'Judo says he's not going to write down anything. But he swears he saw the Marmon at a quarter-to-two near the Grove, which is only about twelve miles out of town.'

'No affidavit,' my father said grimly, disgustedly.

'You're not going to get affidavits against Lockie Mac-Gibbon from anybody,' Tom said firmly. 'Either they like him or they're afraid of him, or rather of Finn MacCooil.'

My father did not comment and we finished dinner in silence, my father chewing vigorously and thinking, my mother watching Tom and easily recognizing some subtle change in him and wondering what it was. Jean my sister was reading a biology book (she wanted to become a doctor and she could do no wrong as far as my father was concerned, even reading at table) and Tom and I were waiting anxiously to get up and get out, but we had to wait until my father put down his napkin. Then we all got up and Tom and I went outside and leaned against the walnut tree where we had always exchanged our information.

Tom was very restless. 'Listen, Kit,' he said to me. 'I can't stand much more of this. I know Lockie set fire to his house, but why should I go around like a policeman trying to prove it?'

'I thought you'd be fascinated,' I said drily. We were on good terms, considering everything, but being the elder and being a compromiser I had a right to be cynical with anything and everything he did.

'Don't be stupid,' he said.

'Then why don't you tell the old man?'

'Tell him what?' Tom said furiously. 'He knows Joe Collins and the police aren't going to suspect Lockie of anything, so he feels he has to do it, and not only for the insurance either.'

'So?'

'You know what's going to happen, don't you?'

'No. Tell me,' I said with mock fascination.

'Oh shut up,' he said. 'The old man is going to collect a bit more evidence of conspiracy and then turn it all over to the State Prosecutor's Office and insist that they do something. And when he does that they know they'll have to act because he knows the law better than they do.'

'But you haven't collected all that much proof.'

'Yes we have. Dorman Walker sent that tin bathtub to Bendigo on one of his grain trucks. The Insurance Company sent it to the analysis laboratory at the Bendigo School of Mines and they say that it was definitely filled with petrol and set alight. That's almost enough to put Lockie in jail.'

'Not here it isn't,' I pointed out.

'Maybe not. But I'll bet the old man thinks up something else. He's going to get Lockie this time. Lockie's going to end up in jail.'

'What are you so worried about?' I asked cunningly.

'I hate the whole bloody thing.'

'Lockie?' I said incredulously.

'Oh, Lockie's an arsonist,' Tom said with a shrug. 'But why should it be me who points it out?'

'The law,' I reminded him.

'I know. But it's getting beyond that.'

'You mean Peggy?' I said tauntingly.

He was stunned. The idea that anyone had seen those brief but lyrical moments between them, and had also correctly interpreted them, had not occurred to him. But that was the difference between Tom and me. Tom lived by breathing, but I lived by touch. Some day, I knew, I was going to put it all down – every strung nerve in my body that saw and felt everything that happened all around me all the time, incessantly. But Tom ate his life, like a man eating an orange, skin and all.

'What about Peggy?' he said aggressively.

'Never mind,' I said. 'But be careful. You can really make trouble there.'

'But I haven't done a thing.'

'Then just be careful,' I repeated mysteriously.

'Ah, you don't even understand,' he growled, which was his usual method of explaining the inexplicable.

He did not tell me so, but I knew he was now going down

to the MacGibbon house by the river in the hope of seeing Peggy. It was a fair hope, because Peggy was sure to be outside looking for Tom. She was, in fact, sitting on the front step of the verandah under our warm Australian sky, staring for luck as we all did at the constellation we all considered our own – the Southern Cross. When Tom went by she knew by instinct where he would go, and she got up and strolled down the path towards the river where Finn Mac-Cooil lived in a house built by his drunken father to resemble the deck-house of his sunken paddle-steamer.

The two of them met half-way along the river path and simply fell into each other's arms as if someone had fired a starting shot as a signal for their tangled lives to begin. Many safe years later I asked Peggy what happened that night and most of what I write here of their intimacy comes from Peggy, not from Tom who hardly said a word about it. Peggy said she could never remember anything of their love-making that night, except that it was aesthetically pure and proper. Though Peggy had flighty eyes and a boy-teasing manner she was scared to death by her religion of any transgression from an unstated but understood norm. *He must not touch me anywhere that matters.* But she said she didn't even think of the rules, although she was never sure whether this was because she trusted Tom or whether she just blindly didn't care about them.

At that age and knowing Peggy, I don't think she cared about them, because women, though permanently constructing newer and subtler defences for their unwanted virtue, are far more courageous in passion than men are, and there was no doubt that in this relationship Peggy had all the courage and was willing to be wild, and it was Tom, who was supposed to be wild, who was scared of going too far, for Peggy's sake.

This rather clinical analysis hardly does them justice

because love was love, even in 1937, and flesh is flesh and what they felt is what we have all felt when we cross that short frontier for the first time and find ourselves in the exotic forests of love from which we never escape again.

'My God, why did you wait so long?' was Peggy's first passionate sentiment.

Tom was stunned. He thought he had been anything but a laggard, forgetting that he had been down at old Dreiser's talking politics when Peggy had been out on Dunlap Street looking for him. 'I'm sorry, Peg,' he said contritely, 'I didn't really know ...' He was hurt by her complaint. All his confidence had suddenly gone.

Peggy groaned in ecstasy. She said she never loved Tom more than when the bottom suddenly dropped out of his blond and blue-eyed and stubborn world. This happened fairly often anyway under normal circumstances, but Peggy quickly learned to augment it, simply as a technique of loving him and enjoying the passionate fury of protecting him and physically smothering him, although it was all unspecified in her wild young mind and only subtly spoken of by her wild young body.

'I'll never let anybody *touch* you!' she cried, squashing her soft willing chest into his. 'I'll *hate* you if you ever touch anyone else. Anyone!'

Tom was a little taken aback by the passion, afraid of finding it so fierce in someone else, because he already had a difficult job disciplining his own desires. He was certainly in love, but it was very much in Tom's character to be terrified of hurting the thing he loved, and for the first time in his life something genuinely dangerous was at war with his over-developed conscience.

'I don't know what we're going to do, Peg,' he said grimly then. 'Everybody's going to be against this. Everybody.'

'I don't care ...'

'I don't either, but what the devil do we do?'

Peggy said : 'Do you love me?'

'Of course . . .'

'Then you must tell me you do.'

'I love you, Peg.'

'That's all I'll ever care about,' she said in happy green-eyed tears.

Considering their situation they had not done too badly. So far there had been very little banality in their situation, although I would like to have heard Tom in his orange-eating way say to Peggy, 'I love you, Peg.' (But I am the Lotus eater, so I can afford to laugh.)

They embraced and squashed each other again and Peggy kept groaning happily to herself for the desire in her soft young breasts which felt everything and knew nothing. Tom's ecstasy was inclined to be pagan and athletic, and he told her afterwards that he felt like lifting her up over his head, arms stretched out to the sky, and walking down to the river with her high over his head and throwing her in and then jumping after her. After all, sex is not all sex.

I think I am in danger of becoming flippant, but twenty-seven years is too long a time to recall the inception of young love with anything but a dry little smile. It was obviously more intense than I make it out to be, and Tom on the way home that night growled and kicked and bit viciously at the world which was hounding him into a dark corner when everything in him wanted to pour down the public streets at a hundred miles an hour with a gay and happy Peg wrapped on his arm. Peggy, brought up in a darker morality than ours, didn't mind the secrecy so much now that the joy had arrived. She could nurture and nurse her passion and protect it and even built on it in her secret heart, and she went home saturated with wonderful discoveries of the body and the good Catholic soul, but she had to hide herself from her knowing mother who would easily recognize what had just innocently happened to her.

The fact that nothing had happened, except that she and Tom had met and embraced and admitted love, was not Peggy's view of it at all. She was secretly so happy that she knew that she must have committed sin, although which one of the seven official measures of deadly sin she wasn't sure of. Peggy had already become a little bored with confession on Fridays, where, in the little three-ply confessional which always smelled of horse manure because it was near the paddock where the country people coming to Mass tied up their buggies, she told Father Flaherty her sins of the week – sometimes one of each of all six of them, because the seventh she had so far not admitted to herself, the seventh being lust. Her sins were all of the highest intellectual sort because the ordinary transgressions against the law of the land, which a daughter of Lockie saw plenty of, did not even come into the category of a sin to be confessed.

But Tom came into the category. Was it *lust*? Was it now the seventh deadly transgression? She was passionately hopeful, but not sure. She only knew he was a sin; and that Friday on her way to Father Flaherty the whole idea of confession, which had so far been a novel and glamorous proof of her womanhood, suddenly became menacing.

She changed her mind at every street corner: *yes I will tell him, no I won't tell him. I dare not!* But even the thought of not telling was sinful so it became complicated and she still had not made up her mind when she went into the old brick church and turned right by the vestry to the confessional box where old Mrs Lightfoot (she was 80; what sins could she possibly have committed?) suddenly emerged. When Peggy sat down under the hot corrugated iron roof and bowed her head and mumbled the preliminaries, Father Flaherty said in his cheerful and already-forgiving voice:

'Well, my child?'

She began the formal, begging appeal: 'I confess to God the Father Almighty, His Only Begotten Son Jesus Christ ...' and confessed formally to sinning exceedingly in thought, word and deed by her own fault, her most grievous fault; but she remained hopelessly undecided until she came to the self-incriminating middle when the sins had to be specified. She confessed to lying to her mother, she had felt envy of her sister, she had indulged in ire with her father, and she had ...

She heard old Father Flaherty sigh. He was bored and hot. He was an affectionate old man who always wanted to laugh at a good joke. This must be hell for him, and anyway he would always forgive you anything because he enjoyed absolving you so long as you mumbled your sins contritely, because contrition was 'the hatred of sin'.

So she told him she had kissed a boy at night, in the darkness, and embraced him.

She heard Father Flaherty sit up and clear his throat.

'What boy, my child? Of the faith?'

'Yes, Father,' she lied. 'It was Finn MacCooil.'

Peggy was sure that behind the curtain Father Flaherty said to himself: 'But Holy Mother – *another* one for Finn MacCooil.'

Peggy giggled for her incredible lie, then she felt real contrition, not only for her lie but for her wicked sense of humour. What had been only a small transgression, kissing Tom, had now become a recognizable and serious sin against God and the Holy Ministry, and a hundred Hail Marys and two shillings in the box and a gentle warning slap on the mental backside from Father Flaherty would not settle her conscience at all.

Why had she told such a terrible lie?

She didn't know, but when she thought about it she

decided that it was her instinct for self-preservation, because she knew that if she told Father Flaherty that she'd been kissing Tom Quayle, Father Flaherty would not of course break the confession but in the interests of the community her father would instantly find out. For the first time in her life Peggy felt that she had really done wrong in the eyes of her Heavenly Father.

For Tom, on the other hand, the idea of confessing a sin to anybody was Protestant anathema, but he suffered in another way because old Dreiser was mentally bleeding him for the agony of Spain, dying brutally in the last days of its civil war.

Old Dreiser had once been a Catholic himself (as a boy in Hamburg) and like all Catholics who deny their faith he always had an open wound on that side of his mind which felt more profoundly anything savage in the Church, in its passionate self-conviction, indulged in. The Church's removal of its sturdy German lower clergy who opposed Hitler, and the failure of Pope Pius XI to interfere when Hitler murdered millions of Jews, became something of an issue twenty-five years later when Hochhuth wrote his play *The Representative*, but it was already well known to all the Hans Dreisers and Tom Quayles at the time.

In fact these were the lessons on political religion that Dreiser was teaching Tom, so Tom hated the political Faith and the political priests as much as he hated Hitler and Mussolini; and the knowledge that it was part of Peggy's religion and Peggy's priesthood that he hated was something he could hardly avoid thinking about.

8

Yet he tried to avoid it. By instinct they both tried to evade all the glaring hatred that was trying to surround them and divide them, naïvely hoping to preserve their secret little world against all the outside interference which was waiting to destroy them. What hope did they really have? Very little, because they could hardly stop their world and get off.

I guessed there was going to be more trouble for them when I went to the Shire Hall where the finals of the singing contests were being sung, and between listening to our local girls Annie Flagg and Dorothy Tate singing, superbly, beautifully, competitive German lieder, song by song, I saw my father at the back of the hall, his head back, entranced by Annie Flagg's sudden change to Handel's *Si, tra i ceppi* (Love that's true will live forever).

There was nothing very unusual about his presence here, because we were all musical. We could not afford a car but we had an excellent gramophone and a good little library of opera and classical records (Purcell began, for my father, all music). He himself played the piano, heavily but well, and so did I, and my sister played the violin and I also played the flute and Tom the oboe (or rather the cor anglais) and we would still gather in the front room and play elementary trios on Sundays. Tom could sing very well but he would only sing now when he was in the bush, and then he would shout songs like 'On the road to Mandalay' trying to sound like Peter Dawson, but the ignorant tree-tops never understood what he was doing to them.

It was therefore normal enough to see my father sitting in the competition hall, but I knew that when he listened to music with his head back and his eyes closed he was making up his mind on some serious legal problem. I wondered what it was, and Tom, on the way home at lunch time, told me that Edward J. Quayle had been asked by the Australasian Univermag Fire Insurance Company to advise them on their reply to Lockie MacGibbon's claim: to give or not to give.

'Isn't the answer obvious?' I said.

Tom twisted his body in the legal way, as if he were already going through the mental hoops of his future profession. 'It looks obvious,' he admitted, 'but if he tells the insurance company to reject Lockie's claim the whole thing can't just stop there.'

'Why not?' I asked. 'Lockie's not going to sue the insurance company, that's sure.'

'No, but a refusal to pay him is as good as a public accusation of arson,' Tom pointed out. 'Anyway the old man is definitely going to ask the company if he can turn everything over to the State Prosecutor's Office.'

'Turn what over?' I asked cynically. 'He hasn't got that much.'

'He's now got his affidavit on Lockie's car that night. He sent me out to see Picky Pickering, you know that Seventh Day religious maniac who collects the Riverside milk for the butter factory at all hours of the night, and he saw Lockie's car coming into town that night, but from the wrong direction. Lockie had deliberately gone right around the town. Anyway, Pickering has signed and sworn his statement.'

'Ah well ...' I sighed. 'How's Peggy taking it?'

Tom's athletic response to love was always fascinating. He leapt up in the air four or five feet, ostensibly to snatch a leaf from one of the overhanging peppercorn trees, but his innocent eyes had also put up a filmy, resentful barrier against me.

'She doesn't know,' he said unhappily. 'We don't talk about it.'

I laughed – to myself, because I wasn't going to risk Tom's swinging fist by laughing in his troubled face.

When we were all having lunch (my father had brought home some Worcester sausages which he had persuaded a local English immigrant sausage-maker to manufacture) there was a rap at the back door and Tom was sent to see who it was.

'It's Sergeant Joe Collins,' Tom said when he came back.

'What does *he* want?' my father asked.

'You,' Tom said, a little meanly I thought, but they were on edge with each other these days for so many reasons.

Fortunately lunch was over otherwise my father would have made the local chief constable wait. He went out and stood at the back door.

'Well, Collins? What is it?'

Australians hate being called by their surnames, and the way my father said *Collins* made it more than a naked surname, it became an insultingly barren handle. (Tom, the Australian, had fought fights for this too – insisting on being called Tom, even by his enemies, not Quayle.)

'It's about Lockie MacGibbon,' Collins said aggressively.

'Don't come here,' my father told him. 'Come to my office.'

Collins was easily undone. 'Actually, Mr Quayle,' he said with reluctant but determined politesse, 'it's unofficial, so I didn't want to come to your office.'

'You've got your uniform on nonetheless,' my father pointed out.

Joe Collins always wore the old trooper's uniform, even in 1937: white doeskin riding breeches, black calf-length boots, black policeman's jacket and pointed policeman's helmet. He still rode a very fine mare (he had arrived on it) and every year in the Anzac Day ceremonies, which were nearer God than any church service ever held in our town, Joe would lead the parade of veterans on his beautifully-limbed Gericault horse which almost broke its back trying to escape the town band, but Joe was a magnificent horseman. The trooper is not a good Australian image, for even in Waltzing Matilda, which is Australia's genuine anthem, the troopers are on the anti-popular side with the squatters.

But Collins loved the old role of the mounted man, although he was a brute on a horse and a coward off it, and we sympathized with my father's proud contempt for him He had once tried to ride my father down when he had taken a client to the police pound to recover two dray horses which had been illegally arrested. The client, a Scotch immigrant, had ducked Joe's horse but my father had stood his ground and he whacked the prancing horse across the mouth and shouted at Collins: 'I shall have you in court, Collins, for juridical reluctance to carry out a magistrate's orders, and for misuse of Her Majesty's (Victoria's) staff and implements . . .'

Collins would not have taken it from any other man, but he took it from my father because he knew in a court he would be mincemeat for laws that my father could think up and even the judges had to consult.

'I'm sorry about the uniform,' Collins mumbled now with some degree of hot-faced pride. 'But I just wondered if you couldn't give Lockie back his bathtub.'

'What bathtub?' my father demanded.

'Why . . . I mean that bathtub that was in Lockie's house.'

'Are you suggesting that *I* have it?'

'Well, somebody's got it, Mr Quayle. Lockie told me . . .'

'Tom,' my father called. 'Bring a pencil and a notepad and take all this down.' He turned back to Collins. 'If you accuse me of having that bathtub, Collins, there are not only laws of defamation but laws of contumely and scornful insolence. Tom, take down everything he says.'

'But you've got a forensic report on it . . .'

'A chemist's report,' my father corrected scornfully. 'I have documents about that bathtub, I have facts about it.'

'Then where is it?'

'Tom, take that down. Implied accusations of conspiracy. He's here as a private citizen, he admits it. Don't you come here asking me where that tin bathtub is, Collins. You're in trouble if you even say another word to me about it.'

'Ah, but it's bloody-well impossible trying to talk to you,' Collins groaned in a moment's grim but helpless temper.

'Tom. Take that down.'

My father was enjoying himself, we all were. Poor Collins. Nobody liked him, not even Lockie who liked every-body. I think Lockie bribed him, or had something on him. Strangely enough we all liked Collins's son, 'Shocker' (he was mad on electricity), who was as clear and as honest as a bell and who eventually gave up electricity and became what must have been a wonderful priest and cricketer.

'But I can't help it,' Collins complained now. 'I'm just . . .'

'You're just doing your duty,' my father finished for him. 'Your duty is not to invade privacy under excuse of office and cause grief and discomfort to Her Majesty's (Victoria's) subjects by interfering in their orderly and lawful behaviour . . .'

Joe Collins fled, and I swear I could hear his teeth grinding as he left.

'Good old dad,' Tom said generously as we came in.

'Pshaw!' My father airily dismissed his victory with his favourite literary sound and a contemptuous wave of the hand. 'It wasn't even law,' he said, as if he wouldn't waste good law on Collins. 'Just words.'

But my mother looked unhappily at him and said, 'Some day, Edward Quayle, that man is going to meet you on a dark night and he'll kill you.'

'If I don't, in fact, kill him first,' my father replied calmly, and they were the most violent words I ever heard him speak in his life, because they were quite outside the law, and that was almost denying God.

'Good on you, Dad,' Tom repeated.

'Don't bring that wretched language in here!' my father growled to cover up his obvious indulgence in a bit of fun.

Good on you was Australian and we were not allowed to speak Australian at home. My father would quote Edward Gibbon Wakefield, who once said that spoken Australian was the corrupted slang of English thieves, so Tom and I had to speak two languages – English at home. and the thieves' language outside among our mates where my father couldn't hear it. Yet over the years he had acquired a very slight Australian twang himself, although he would have gone to the moon if we had told him so.

But it was clear from Joe Collins's visit that Lockie was becoming anxious and perhaps a little desperate. However, there was one last detail my father wanted and Tom, even while he was falling into the arms of Peggy MacGibbon every night by Finn MacCooil's deck-house, had to collect it.

A knowledge of our town and of the affection ('false', of course) for Lockie which many people had, made my father hesitate to ask for statements from townspeople. He was very clever to wait, because he knew that if he had immediately asked any of our volunteer firemen or Lockie's neighbours what their view of the fire was, they would all have given Lockie a clean slate. But my father waited for the town to hear all the fascinating rumours about sworn affidavits and chemical analyses of the tin bathtub. Friends would shout at me in the street these days: 'Hello, Kit. How's the bathtub?' Everybody soon suspected that my father had plenty of proof of Lockie's guilt. And because there wasn't a man in the town who wouldn't watch his step when dealing with my father under these circumstances it was a good tactic to allow the rumours to spread and then ask the firemen and the neighbours for the truth.

There was no clean slate for Lockie now. The amateur firemen gave Tom very cautious statements, so cautious that they really pointed the finger of guilt at Lockie MacGibbon. In Australia big fire insurance companies like the Univermag contributed heavily to the upkeep of local fire brigades, including ours in St Helen, and our firemen did not want to have trouble with their patrons. The chief fireman was a baker named 'Muscles' Smith – a body-building disciple of the great Sandow. Muscles insisted that you could actually hear his muscles whispering when he walked, and Muscles admitted that the fire seemed to have started at the back where the bathroom was, and that it probably began on the floor rather than on the roof.

The next-door neighbour, a sick draper whom Lockie had sometimes helped, and strangely enough so had my father, admitted that the fire seemed to have started in the back of the house, near the bathroom to be exact. He had also heard a 'whoosh' as if something had ignited fiercely. Tom had been told to ask that question. Both these statements denied Peggy's version that the fire had started in the roof, so it was clear that potential witnesses were now afraid of what my father could do to them in court if they were ever called to give evidence.

Tom, however, was in agony.

He tried to persuade Peggy one night to swim the river with him and go wandering around the Billabong. The bush along the river was Tom's private monastery – a momentary escape from the town, but Peggy told him he was mad.

'Why?' he said fiercely.

'We won't be back for hours,' she pointed out, 'and they'll miss me.'

'Ah, I just wanted to get away from the town,' Tom said disgustedly.

'Darling!' Peggy said and embraced him.

For someone like Peggy to secretly call you *Darling* in those days, and in darkness, was almost erotic and Tom must have felt like jumping the river rather than swimming it. Yet he would not say *Darling* himself.

'Peg,' he said. 'I can't stand much more of this.'

'Of what, darling,' Peggy said lovingly as they clung to each other under one of the big sheltering peppercorn trees with crickets and frogs and fireflies and jumping fish and barking dogs and some far-off laughter in the night as local orchestration for them.

'Your father and mine.'

Peggy, dreaming bodily in the arms of a lover who did not touch her where it mattered, but whose body was none the less flagrantly in love with hers, felt all her nourishing eroticism disintegrate.

'Don't even *talk* about that!' she warned Tom sharply.

Tom threw his hands helplessly in the air and said grimly:
'We have done with Hope and Honour, so we are lost to Love and Truth . . .'

'What?' Peggy had not been educated on Kipling's drum.

'There's going to be a lot of trouble,' Tom said.

Peggy shook her long red hair. 'I know! But don't talk about it. I don't want to hear.'

'What's the use of not talking about it?' Tom said determinedly.

'All right. But why does your father want to persecute mine?'

'Oh, they hate each other,' Tom said calmly. 'Why does Lockie do such stupid things?'

'I don't know, Tom,' Peggy said unhappily. 'He can't help it I suppose.'

They were silent.

'Lockie shouldn't have come back that night.'

'What night?' Peggy said.

'The night of the fire.'

'He didn't come back,' Peggy said indignantly. 'He never came near the place. He was in Nooah all night . . .'

'But . . .'

Tom told me afterwards that he didn't really believe her. He assumed that she had to maintain the lie for Lockie's sake, so he didn't go on with it. She was being a good daughter and protecting her father. In any case she firmly forbade any more talk of it.

'I'm not going to talk about it,' she informed him. 'And you're not either. You're not to talk about it!' she commanded.

'All right,' he said. 'But . . .'

'No!' she cried.

Tom said no more and they fell into each other's arms again. What else could they do? But he wished later on, in the light of everything that happened, that he had pursued it to the end that night.

The next day my father advised the Univermag Insurance Company to refuse Lockie's claim on the grounds of reasonable doubt about the origin of the fire. There were many factors which suggested 'carelessness far beyond legitimate causes', and there had been 'deliberate or wilful or conscious acts which could have led to the destruction of said structure in an unlawful manner'. The Company accepted his advice and my father wrote the letter to Lockie for Dorman Walker. But the Company did not agree that all information should be turned over to the State Prosecutor. Not yet anyway. The Company would give that more thought.

So Lockie had a breather, but I knew my father well enough to know that he would willingly risk his business with the big insurance companies and hand his information over to the authorities if he thought it legally necessary and morally right. Although for some reason, probably because he hated the idea of hounding a man on whom he had such an advantage, he too hesitated.

9

The trouble was that Tom and Peggy took the lull too literally because they became careless, or perhaps it was inevitable anyway that someone should see them together and begin the kind of rumour which was always the heart-beat of our respectable town.

At that time I was light-mindedly courting the station-master's daughter, and though Grace Gould was probably the most attractive girl in the town and the pleasantest I was not being serious because I knew that generous destiny was somehow going to take me far away from a small-town future, and I had no intention of becoming too involved with such a serious girl. Grace was studying to be a herd tester and veterinary for the Department of Agriculture, although she wanted to be a doctor which she could not afford to become. What I didn't know was she thought the same thing about me as I thought about her, and she gave me no more than fingertip love because she did not want *my* small-town future. She would do better, and she probably did.

Grace, dark-eyed and olive-boned and olive-skinned, told me one Saturday night as we sat down in the Pentagon Café eating tutti-frutti (one-eighth of my week's salary) that Tom had been seen at night with Peggy MacGibbon under the peppercorns by the MacCooil deck-house.

'Can it really be true?' she asked slyly.

'Who saw them?' I said cautiously.

'My father,' Grace said calmly.

That was a blow. I could hardly doubt his word, although I didn't like him much, though for no reason except that he was Grace's father.

'What was your father doing down there at night?' I said aggressively, anxious to defend Tom.

'He has a crawfish net in the river near the engine-sheds,' Grace said.

I had to accept the inevitable. 'Yes, it's true,' I said, weighing myself heavily with the responsibility of it. 'They're up to their eyes in each other.'

Grace laughed. 'I've never heard anything so funny in my life.' She was incredulous now that it was confirmed. 'What's your father going to say?'

'I hope to God he never finds out.'

'But someone else will surely see them.'

'Then they'll have to take their punishment,' I said.

'Lockie MacGibbon will kill Tom if he finds out.'

'Agreed,' I said glumly.

'Are they in love?' she asked in the way that only a woman can ask a man to commit himself about love, even about someone else's love.

'Madly,' I said.

'Poor Tom,' Grace said affectionately, and I knew she had pictured Tom's untainted blue eyes that needed her protection. It was amazing, it never failed. I looked at my own eyes in the mirror that night to see if I had any hint of this desperate need to be looked after, but my eyes mocked me with a worldly awareness of their frustrated lack of twenty-year-old sex appeal.

When I got home late that night Tom was sitting on the front step of the verandah, and I warned him that he'd actually been seen. 'And if the old man hears about it,' I added, 'he'll disinherit you dead or alive.'

'Don't worry,' Tom growled.

'And what about Peggy?' I went on. 'What'll Lockie say or rather what'll he do if he finds out?'

'To Peggy?'

'Yes.'

'God, I don't know. It's frightening.'

'He'll probably set Finn MacCooil on you.'

'Finn doesn't frighten me,' Tom said.

'Finn hasn't been brought up to be an English gentleman,' I reminded him cynically. 'So watch out when your back is turned.'

'I tell you I'm not afraid of Finn,' Tom said angrily, implying that I ought to mind my own bloody business. I did. I didn't pursue it.

Tom was out of sorts anyway because he had just quarrelled with Peggy. She had expected him to join the Dunlap Street Saturday night parade, now that they could pass each other like blind butterflies in the night and exchange secret green and blue messages across the public footways.

I had watched Peggy myself that night from the café. She had walked up and down Dunlap Street once, and for a while she stood helplessly by the Salvation Army band who were playing outside the Sunshine Hotel. Three or four youths I had been at school with were drunkenly singing vulgar words to the well-known Salvation hymns, but the Salvation Army, who were used to this sport (although I must say that they asked for it) foxed their mockers by leaving the hymns alone and playing the song that Lensky sings to Olga in *Eugene Onegin: Olga I love you . . . I love thee.* I wondered if the trumpeter who played it knew what it was or what it meant. Obviously not. It was the music he was passionately in love with. The trumpeter was a musical carpenter named Foam. He was not a local man but a salvationist specially imported to strengthen the band, and the suppressed silver tone on his B flat trumpet has never had any equal for me in my life, and as I strolled down warm Dunlap Street under one of Australia's spangled blue nights with Grace Gould by my side and Eugene Onegin's aristocratic Russian love ringing very old bells in our brand new air, I was hopelessly in love with every woman in the street, even Peggy whom I passed and whose green eyes looked at me reproachfully as if I were to blame for Tom's absence.

This was all happening before their subsequent quarrel, and at the time that Peggy was looking for him Tom was grieving with Hans Dreiser on the latest news from Spain. Anthony Eden had just agreed to an 'exchange of agents' with Franco, which amounted to recognition of an illegal government even while the civil war was still going on. Attlee had protested, but Eden had reassured him that it was only for convenience. Hans Dreiser and Tom knew, of course, as Attlee knew that it was simply a British convenience to compromise with Franco, who was being put into power by German and Italian bombers and by Eden's twisting policy of appeasement. They ate figs from Dreiser's garden and stared glumly across the Billabong at the fascist future.

Tom longed to go to Spain and fight with the Republicans, and old Dreiser had told him how it had been at the end of the First World War in Germany when soldiers and workers had marched through the streets of all the German cities with red armbands on their sleeves and with long-bayoneted rifles over their shoulders bringing an old and vicious order to an end, except that it had been reimposed on them ten years later and worse. Revolution in 1920, Dreiser said, meant not only the Russian revolution but European revolution. All Europe had been on fire then, and all Europe in 1937 was still on fire with the same revolution and the same enemy, although the enemies were now building a vast machinery of destruction without parallel in history. Tom listened to all this music and knew every Saturday night that the time was coming when he would have to go and face it. He would have to go to war to stop this monster eating up the world. Even I felt it distantly, no matter how determinedly detached I kept myself. I knew through some unguarded nerve that my ripest years were going to be spent fighting a war; and I think even the stupidest boy in the town suspected it, although only Tom knew why and what for.

That was the big burden on Tom's conscience late on Saturday night when he met Peggy and locked arms, lips, ears and knees in the sort of embrace that Peggy said she could never really remember afterwards because they simply melted into each other like jelly.

'But where were you tonight?' Peggy demanded when they managed to separate.

'At Hans Dreiser's,' Tom said.

'That awful and filthy old man. What do you see in him?'

Tom took the blow with his feet firmly on the ground. Hans was anything but filthy, in fact if you walked into the engine-sheds and watched him at work he was always organized and meticulous and clean, even when he was dirty, and my memory of him is of a vocationally devoted mechanic efficiently in love with the inside of an A3 steam locomotive.

'He's not filthy, Peg,' Tom said stiffly.

'Well his *mind* is,' Peggy said.

Peggy was feeling frustrated from Dunlap Street, and Tom was feeling frustrated because he was in St Helen and not in Spain with a rifle and long bayonet marching up some dusty white Spanish road singing International Brigade songs in German and drinking Andalusian wine from a pitch-lined leather bottle.

'You're wrong,' Tom said firmly.

'*You're wrong . . .*' she mimicked.

'He's a remarkable old man,' Tom insisted.

'I don't want you to even talk to him. I don't want you to even go near him again,' Peggy said decisively. 'I mean it!'

Tom was suddenly facing a dilemma he had not expected: love versus politics, or love versus ideology, or love versus what you really think you are. He was at a disadvantage for once, because it was so dark that Peggy could not see his defenceless face. No doubt if she had seen his face she would have flung her arms around him and begged his forgiveness. Unfortunately, Tom was blacked out from the moon by the fractious shadows.

'But you don't even know him,' Tom pointed out. 'So what have you got against him?'

'Everybody knows he wants to blow everything up,' Peggy replied.

'That's silly,' Tom said.

That was careless of him. The serious picture of the Bolshevik in 1937 was the *Punch* version of the bearded Russian carrying an unexploded bomb. Additionally Father Flaherty had already warned every young Catholic against the Godless menace of Hans Dreiser, the devil's advocate who enticed the innocent and the faithful into the paths of self-destruction and denial of God.

'I won't talk to you again if you go *near* him,' Peggy cried fiercely.

Tom tried to keep his head. 'What if I said I didn't want you to go to Mass again.'

'*Tom!*'

'But it's the same.'

'What an *awful* thing to say.' Peggy clapped her hands over her ears to blot it out.

'But it means exactly the same to me.'

74

'I can't love you now! I can never love you if you talk like that.'

'But it does mean exactly the same to me,' Tom replied miserably. 'Honestly . . .'

'That's *awful*.' Peggy was so horrified that she began to walk away, to leave him, and she walked straight into Finn MacCooil. She and Tom had forgotten their cunning way of listening for other footsteps on that path.

'Peggy!' Finn said. 'Well I'll be buggered. What are you doing here?'

Peggy smacked his face in her fury and surprise, and since Finn was more drunk than not he was so stunned that he laughed in embarrassment. But Peggy said to him: 'If you ever tell my father, Finn, I'll never talk to you again. And I'll tell everything I know about you, I swear it.' Peggy ran wildly up the path.

Tom then emerged from the darkness like an iron ghost and Finn, dazed and dizzy, saw his flashing legs and flaying arms go by and he wasn't quite sure . . . maybe it was . . . who was it? But Finn would never know what had happened to him in those five seconds.

Tom caught Peggy at the top of the path. 'Listen . . .' he began.

'No!'

They were already under the street lamps because they were on the real footpath by now. That might explain it, because Peggy must have seen his face and succumbed. She told me she never remembered what did it, but she fell sobbing into Tom's arms and Tom just groaned the way he had to groan. Then they realized they were exposed to the town, nakedly in love, and Peggy fled down the road in terror and ran into her house without looking back, leaving Tom to straddle a thin new chasm between love and his conscience.

*

I did not know at the time what Peggy and Tom had quarrelled about but I guessed it when the next Saturday came around again that Tom was obviously making up his mind about something. He was up long before dawn and had gone over the river to the Billabong with his rifle, and he came back at lunch with six hares which he skinned and four good-sized Murray cod which he sold to the Sunshine Hotel for 8s. 6d. Tom was always successful with his hunting and fishing when he had some big problem on his mind. I suppose the nervous concentration must have made him more alert.

I got an inkling of the trouble when he said to me at six o'clock:

'Are you going down to Dunlap Street?'

'No,' I told him. 'I'm going to see Grace at the Pentagon Café.'

'That's the same thing,' Tom said irritably. 'If you see Peggy somewhere, will you tell her quietly that I'll see her at the usual place at the usual time tonight.'

'All right,' I said, wondering in my ignorance why the message was necessary.

Almost the first person I saw in Dunlap Street was Peggy, on the arm of her beautiful mother.

'Good evening, Mrs MacGibbon,' I said. 'Good evening, Peggy.'

'Hello, Kit,' Mrs MacGibbon said firmly, and I admired her largesse. She was not going to take out on me what she felt about my father, although I knew there would be an understandable limit to her generosity if she knew about Tom and her daughter.

Though I was meeting Grace and I knew she was waiting in the café for me, I fluttered an elaborate message at Peggy with my left eye to indicate something unusual, and before I had gone very far Peggy was suddenly walking near me saying:

'What's the matter?'

'Tom says come to the same place, same time,' I mumbled quickly.

'Did he go down to Hans Dreiser's tonight?'

'I don't know,' I said, although I suspected that he had.

Peggy went into the post office and walked out again and went back to her mother, and I joined Grace for my tutti-frutti. She looked at me suspiciously when I came in.

'Did you just go into the pub for a drink?' she said.

'Me?'

'Yes. I saw you go up that way.'

'I went to the post office,' I lied. I wasn't going to explain my contact with Peggy, because Peggy was only two years younger and quite eligible for my attentions, so I kept my counsel.

'Why don't you ever go to the pub?' Grace asked.

I knew she was teasing me. 'Because it's a big swill,' I said.

I knew that Tom and I had a good-bad reputation for our strict refusal to go into the pub. Australian mateship soaked in hot beer had never attracted either of us so we were considered a little bit too removed for our own good. The curious thing is that my father thought nothing of bringing home an occasional bottle of cheap Australian wine, which was excellent, and which we would have at supper, but most beer-drinking Australians considered this an erotic and evil kind of drinking and shunned it.

But Grace was only kidding me, because that was what we did most of so that we would never become serious with each other even by accident.

When I saw Tom late that night I asked him if he had seen Peggy.

'No, she didn't turn up,' he said laconically.

She did not turn up the Sunday night either, or the Monday or the Tuesday. But on Wednesday she came to the path. It was obvious because Tom was on fire again, and now that I had guessed that they had been arguing about Dreiser, I wondered how Peggy had settled her conscience on that score.

She told me eventually how difficult it was. She was determined not to give in to Tom, and Tom was not able to give in to her because more than his life was at stake. Hans Dreiser had opened up too many doors and windows which offered him world-shaking vistas. Religion and ideology were therefore locked by the horns.

At that time Peggy was planning and training to become a dancing teacher, which was very important to her because this would always prevent any thought in her father's head that she should be the one to go off to the Convent of the Sisters of Charity in Castlemaine to become a nun. Peggy was passionately identified with her dancing, and because the big competitions in Highland dancing were due the following week, she was spending most of her time rehearsing with Mrs Craig Campbell, who knew instantly that Peggy's heart was elsewhere. Peggy would never be able to concentrate on the highly conventional figurations of the Highland dance if she were not thoroughly at peace and enjoying what she was doing.

'There's something wrong,' Mrs Campbell had said to her. 'Are you accursed?'

'No,' Peggy said.

'Then you're sick. Or you're in love. Something's wrong.'

Peggy had denied everything, but she also knew she would never perform adequately if she did not solve this problem of Tom and the Godless influence of Hans Dreiser.

It was a bad situation, but young women have a very good strategic relationship with God, although they usually get into more tactical trouble with Him than men do. They also make huge private deals with Him, outside the dogmatic

78

constitution of any Church, and this particularly applies to young Catholic girls who know very well how to get on with Him, and how to trust His judgement.

So Peggy made a private deal with God which got around the situation. She swore on her prayer book that she would remain chaste, she would never allow Tom to touch her golden body illicitly or improperly if He would permit her to see Tom even though he went on seeing Hans Dreiser. Agreed? Agreed! This was a fair exchange, her purity for His indulgence. After all, she pointed out, Tom was honest and true, and not himself the devil's advocate, so she wasn't really sinning against the first commandment.

On Wednesday morning she made her bargain, and on Wednesday night she went to the path and met Tom who had gone there faithfully every night.

'I won't insist, I won't argue with you,' she said, holding him off so that she made her terms first, 'but you're not allowed to talk to me about that man or about religion or say any of those awful things you said the other night. Do you promise?'

'I promise,' Tom said meekly.

'All right . . .' she said. But they could never finish discussing anything so profound because they would fall on each other's necks and ears and eyes again. Years and years of trouble had passed, love had been brutally threatened, life had barely survived. What a terrible time.

But now it was over and Peggy knew that she would dance very well next Tuesday.

Tom was also satisfied. Hadn't he won his point? But in fact he never went to Hans Dreiser's again without feeling very guilty about it, so Peggy's private God must have laughed his head off, knowing that He got the best of it after all; although what He gained on Tom he probably lost on Lockie.

When Lockie received Dorman Walker's refusal to pay, he took the news very well at first although its real effect on him was not seen until the following week. But what he did that Sunday, though not one of his blackest deeds, upset my father's usual ideas of what was morally and legally allowed in the town.

On most Sundays Lockie ran an illegal two-up school in the green fields just over the town bridge on the New South Wales side of the river. Australian states are ruled jealously by their own state governments and they have their own state laws and state police, and one lot of state police can't operate in any other state. Victorian policemen in St Helen could not cross the river, technically, except as private citizens, and since the nearest town and police force in New South Wales were several hundred miles away, anybody could safely break the gaming and drinking laws just over the bridge in full sight of St Helen's police station and nobody could or would do anything about it, particularly Sergeant Joe Collins. There was even a pub near the bridge on the New South Wales side, the Lightfoot Hotel, where on Sundays, or at any hour of the day or night, you could get an illegal alcoholic drink.

Lockie's Sunday two-up schools just over the bridge were raided about once every year by New South Wales police travelling 200 miles, and someone was fined, but never Lockie. Lockie had once promoted Sunday football just over the bridge, and Sunday plumpton (greyhound coursing with live hares) but this Sunday, after the usual session of two-up, Lockie's wits had invented another diversion which could make him a little money.

He had announced on the local radio station last thing on Saturday night (as an event, not an advertisement) that Dobey the Diver was going to perform one of his rare plunges from the ninety-five-foot high drawbridge into the river on Sunday morning. Everybody who heard it, and the whole town heard of it, knew that if Lockie had announced the event you were going to have to pay to see it. It was doubly interesting because we all knew about Dobey's broken wrist, which was still in dirty white plaster.

'The Victorian police'll have to stop him on the bridge,' Tom said. 'It's illegal on Sunday.'

'Half the bridge belongs to New South Wales,' I pointed out.

'But the people will have to come from our side to see it,' Tom argued.

Lockie was a clever showman and he knew that half the town was arguing along the same lines, curious to see how he would get around several problems. There was no church for us that Sunday, Tom because he had finished with it and I because I was doing my reporter's duty, and anyway good Catholics had already been to early Mass, which meant Lockie and his whole family. They were a very attractive family when you saw them all together on their way to church.

When we got to the bridge there was a considerable crowd, and Lockie had organized a very simple but effective trick to get around the law. On the bridge there were four high towers which held the heavy cables which pulled the middle of the bridge up when a river boat wanted to go through. One of these towers could only be seen from the

New South Wales side, and it was from this one that Dobey would make his dive. Anybody wanting to see the dive would first have to cross the bridge to the New South Wales side where they would have to pay a fee to get into the quite illegal enclosure which Lockie had roped off.

I paid nothing (reporter) and Tom paid a shilling to Finn MacCooil who was collecting the money, and we sat down on the mud-bank on the New South Wales side and watched Dobey with a broken wrist awkwardly climb the iron ladder which went up the wooden tower.

'Ladies and gentlemen, your attention please!'

Lockie was standing at the foot of the tower with a mega-phone, and he began to prepare us for what was about to happen. Dobey the Diver was going to climb to the top. See, he was already half-way up. When he reached the top he would stand on one of the wide wheels on which the cables were rolled up. There he would balance, then he would plunge death-defyingly the ninety-five feet into twelve feet of Murray River below.

'What about his wrist?' I asked.

Everybody could see the white cast, you could see that Dobey was not using his right hand to help him with the rungs of the iron ladder.

'And what's the point of it anyway? It's silly,' Estelle Smith said to us. Estelle was still a tomboy, aged nineteen, and would remain one into sad, puzzled Lesbianism.

'Dobey needs the money,' Tom said laconically.

That was obvious. Two hundred people sat around us on the dry mud of the river bank in the Sunday morning sun. That meant about £10, and if Dobey got a pound for his dive it was a good morning's work.

'Watch, ladies and gentlemen,' Lockie shouted. 'Silence, please.'

We watched.

'Note the overhead high tension wires which Dobey has to avoid.'

Lockie only had to mention the high tension wires to remind everybody of Spike Runciman who, ten months before, had tried to emulate Dobey's feat. At the very moment when he had begun his plunge Spike had panicked and put out his hands and grabbed the high tension wires in terror, electrocuting himself. It was Dobey who had climbed up and brought Spike's body down when they had switched off the current. We all felt the danger now because those wires were a menacing presence for anyone up there who felt a sudden panic as he plunged off the top, even Dobey.

'Quiet!' Lockie roared.

Everybody stopped talking. Dobey was lifting his feet, one after the other, as if drying them or getting a better grip. He was nervous. He did not look down. He looked straight ahead. He waited a long time and someone shouted: 'Get on with it, Dobey!' and Lockie bellowed 'Shut up' to the barracker.

Dobey slowly raised his arms shoulder high, scraped his feet once more, lifted back his head and literally fell forward in a lightly bent position, his arms swinging out like wings.

Women screamed, thinking he had fallen accidentally, but we knew it was his only way of keeping his body flat to prevent it turning over. His legs seemed lower than his head as he plunged down, but at the very moment when it looked as if he were going to hit the water like a broken bird, he straightened up his legs and swung his arms over his head and went into the river with a huge splash which he sucked into the water after him.

Dobey's quiet face bobbed up almost immediately, as if he had barely gone under at all.

We sighed and we cheered.

'Good old Dobey,' Tom said feelingly. 'What a man!'

Everybody was satisfied. Dobey was too shy even to wave a hand, and he turned over on his back and used his legs to swim to the shore. Lockie's voice was drowned by the shouts of encouragement and praise.

'What a disgusting display,' Estelle Smith said angrily, 'it's a wonder he didn't break his wrist again.'

'Maybe he did,' Tom said sharply.

But now that I had seen it I also resisted the whole idea because it seemed to me a miserable exhibition of a physical threat, a calculated exposure to titivate an unhealthy appetite. But Tom was too proud of Dobey to see anything else in it but genuine courage, and though we argued fiercely about it on the way home, Tom said that if your mind couldn't force your body to do what it must do, or was afraid to do, then what was the point in having a mind at all?

'But where's the civilizing discipline,' I asked, 'if the mind simply tells you to do something reckless and stupid?'

'The civilizing discipline is to know thyself,' Tom said decisively, 'and Dobey knows himself.'

That sounded like the remnant of the Berkleyan 'inner compulsion', but Tom would not change his view of Dobey as a man of great mental discipline and wonderful inner strength, so much so that I was worried that in his admiration Tom might attempt the feat himself. But I need not have worried because there were too many other things coming up that would compel Tom to prove his own kind of inner strength and courage without diving off the town bridge.

At lunch, when my father heard of Lockie's Sunday sideshow he said very bitterly: 'That man flaunts the law so openly that there might as well be no law at all. He's making a laughing stock of all of us.' And he added upwards: 'Are there no social attitudes of any kind left in this country?'

'No, none!' Tom said. 'That's what you won't admit . . .'

We were spared an angry argument by a blast of scorching wind which almost lifted our large wooden house off its flimsy foundations. It had been a hot, sultry day and we knew there was going to be a dust-storm. We had seen the black clouds piling up to the north-east over the Darling Downs even as we came home, and now the wall of dust had suddenly hit the town and we leapt up and ran around closing windows and latching doors as the dry grimy tornado of mallee top-soil darkened the house, the street, the whole town, blinding everything, blotting us out.

It would last for days, and then it would rain, and I was never so determined to leave St Helen as now, when the wide open plains, the bush, the river, the mallee acres of sacred wheat and the sight of humanity itself were all locked away in a fog of dust. The town had become a prison, and that is when I always saw what the town really meant and what it was doing to us all, and I made up my mind that day that I would leave St Helen before the next year was out, even if I had to walk out with my swag on my back.

II

The first crack in Lockie's gambler's façade came the following week when he sold his silver Marmon – his streaky bullet. We had always admired the Marmon because it was expensive and dramatic and the most powerful car in town, and it suited Lockie's character. Lockie had suffered his ups and downs before, he had often been nearly destitute, but he had never reached the point of selling the Marmon. Originally he had turned up with it one day four years ago and nobody knew where or how he had got it. It must have been legal because there was no other way he could operate it, but everybody had a different theory about it and the most popular one was that it had been stolen in Queensland and sold to Lockie for nothing by a friend on the run.

It was hard to imagine Lockie without the Marmon or the Marmon without Lockie. The local bicycle shop-owner had bought it, the man who had invented the name 'mudface' for my father.

The next evening Dorman Walker came to our house with a letter delivered by hand to him from a rival barrister and solicitor named J. B. Strapp, informing Dorman Walker in sticky legal language that he was being sued by Lockie for failure to meet the promises and obligations of his insurance contract. Dorman Walker had already had several legal letters from Strapp demanding payment to Lockie, but my father had told him to ignore them.

My father laughed incredulously. 'The fellow's mad,' he said.

'But . . .' Dorman Walker began.

'Typical Australian bluster,' my father went on. '*Brutem fulmen.*'

'But surely he knows he hasn't a chance,' Dorman Walker said nervously, already not sure and appealing for reassurance.

'Out of the frying pan into the legal fire,' my father said pleasantly.

'Are you sure?'

'The State Statutes are something Lockie MacGibbon hasn't been able to corrupt yet, Walker, although who knows in this country?' My father's eyes went to heaven where the grim prospect was once more thrown at the foot of the Great Judge.

'Then why is he doing it?' Walker asked miserably.

'Ask MacGibbon,' my father replied. 'Don't ask me.'

'But you told me to ignore those letters.'

'Did you want to pay MacGibbon?' my father said indignantly. 'If so then pay him.'

'I don't want to pay him. But what do I do now?'

'Consult your superiors first,' my father suggested. 'Then if you want me to defend the case I'll find out from Strapp when he intends to bring it to the county court.'

Dorman Walker wriggled out of his chair. 'I'll turn it all over to the Company,' he said. 'Let them handle it.'

My father tapped the letter from J. B. Strapp. 'But he's not suing the Company, he's suing you as their agent. This is quite specific.'

'Can he do that?' Walker said in a panic.

'He *is* doing it,' my father pointed out.

'But surely the Company will have to take some of the responsibility.' Dorman Walker's wizened voice and wizened face reminded me of a mouse trapped in one of his own granaries.

'That's why I told you to consult the Company first,' my father said. 'They may suggest someone else, not me. But it's you he's suing, not them.'

'That's very unfair!' Dorman Walker groaned as he left. 'And it isn't right. It simply is not right . . .'

'It's not supposed to be right and it's not supposed to be wrong. It's his privilege,' my father pointed out. 'Although he's as game as Ned Kelly for trying it on.'

'But it's not right. Lockie MacGibbon set that house on fire and everybody knows he did,' Dorman Walker said and faded unhappily away.

But my father was far from being unhappy with the possibilities now before him, in fact he seemed delighted. Like Tom, he always wanted to come to grips with an open enemy, and here he was, marching as to war at last.

'But what the devil made him do it?' Tom asked. 'He hasn't got a chance.'

'Strapp has obviously advised him,' my father said. 'But MacGibbon is also being clever. He is probably suing Walker so that he brings the issue into open court on *his* terms. If I had handed all our information over to the State Prosecutor, MacGibbon would have been charged and put into the dock and fought his case on the defensive. This way he obviously hopes to forestall any prosecution.'

'That's a wild hope,' I said. 'Can't you hand over all the information to the Prosecutor's office anyway?'

'Yes, but I won't. It's bad law to make a second issue like that. Strapp knows it. Strapp thinks he's got me on the defensive.' My father smiled like a man finally coming to judgement. 'But we'll see about that.'

'Why is he suing Walker and not the Company?' Tom said.

'He doesn't want to take on the Univermag Insurance Company in Bendigo,' my father pointed out. 'But he doesn't mind taking on little Dorman Walker in a local court sitting in a place where he is well known and well liked. Strapp will try for a jury, but I won't have that.'

I already knew that Lockie's claim, £500, was the maximum amount allowed as an issue in any case before that local County Court. Any sum larger than that and the case would have gone to a higher court outside the town.

'Tom,' my father said. 'Tomorrow look up the CLR (Commonwealth Law Review) Victorian High Court, some time in December I think 1934, and there's a Mildura case under the name of Phillips the appellant . . .'

That was, I suppose, the first legal shot fired by my father in what became a famous and somewhat sad battle in the history of our town. J. B. Strapp put the suit up for the February sessions, and that gave both sides plenty of time to prepare their forces. It also gave Tom and Peggy more time to commit further indiscretions.

Jeannie had heard about them now from one of the girls at school, and she said to Tom: 'It's disgusting. Why did you have to pick Peggy MacGibbon of all people?'

'Mind your own business,' Tom replied.

'It *is* my business . . .'

'Well shut up then,' Tom said fiercely.

'Father will kill you if he finds out.'

'Nobody's going to kill me,' Tom said. 'And what's the matter with Peggy?'

'Nothing,' Jeannie said, her pink face brick-red with purpose. 'But she's not for you. You're being selfish. Look what Lockie did to father at the hospital fête, and now they're about to murder each other in court. You ought to think of him sometimes. You make it more difficult for him.'

Tom had obviously not thought of that aspect of it, and neither had I, but we could both see the truth in it. Tom's face was like a magic lantern: his conscience was now whipping up the troubled surface of his mind. Could love be so selfish? Yes, it could be so selfish, there was no doubt about it.

'You're childish and thoughtless,' Jeannie said, as if she had read his mind the way I had.

Unfortunately my mother came on our family consultation under the walnut tree at this moment, and she said: 'What on earth are you two quarrelling about? The neighbours will hear every word.'

We were all inclined to shout in an argument, and sometimes we had very bitter family quarrels when we all shouted at the same time. To an outsider we would probably sound worse than we really were, although sometimes we did hurt each other badly. But we always made it a strict rule that no matter how we felt and what we said it was all finished with next day. The old Judaic 'vengeance is mine, and recompense' was not allowed.

'Oh, to hell with the neighbours,' Jeannie said to my mother.

'Jeannie! If your father heard your language...'

Jeannie was so hot-tempered that I thought she was going to tell my mother about Tom and Peggy. I knew Tom wouldn't stop her simply out of pride, so I intervened.

'Jeannie is speculating, Mama, on the kind of girl who is good enough for Tom. So far there aren't any.'

'Don't be silly,' my mother said.

The idea of Tom with a girl was probably natural, but the realization that we were all becoming young adults was cracking my mother. Closed in the exiled dream of small brown brooks and crumbling abbeys and tiny glens, she wondered more and more often these days what she was doing out here on our dry hot plains. We all saw it in her struggling eyes; we knew that at the moment she was just giving up all hope of ever seeing home again and we tried not to upset her or make her job of holding the household together financially more difficult. I had settled into a sort of calming explanation of the world for her, Tom was always lightly teasing her, and Jeannie was firmly forthright. Tom alone could stir her to fun, and only a few weeks ago he had provoked her just enough to have her chase him outside and down the pathway under the grapevines with a broom in her hand shouting at him: 'You devil, Tom Quayle. You shibi devil!' My mother always came from some other time, some other land.

We sat around now under the walnut tree on a big black mallee stump which some day Tom swore he would chop up for firewood when we got low on fuel. It was his job to chop enough wood every night to keep the kitchen fire going all next day. Beside the old log there was a rough bench and a hammock, and in the hot summer afternoons it was cool and pleasant. It was my mother who had begun this habit of sitting under the walnut tree, mainly I think because it was not a eucalypt or a wattle tree or anything indigenous.

My father had turned on the radio and we could hear *The Marriage of Figaro* sifting like fine musical dust through the thin curtains of the living-room. He came down and joined us and sat in his waistcoat smoking a pipe, which he did sometimes, and read the Melbourne papers of the day before. Jeannie was going tum-tte-ttte doo-doo to the music, and the hot afternoon simply held off, held itself high up in the faint blue sky as if giving us a moment of pleasure, or at least a lucky moment of hesitation between the awful acts of life.

I suppose we looked like a happy family, and on the whole

we were, except that Tom and my father were now permanently watching each other with a dangerously neutral eye, and Tom had in his hip pocket the book that was teaching him to indict the world: Lenin's *State and Revolution*. My own book, my unfinished expedition into some unfinished future, was still in my head. It was going to be written in the Russian manner and called *The Outback Diary of a Faint Heart*. I was the *Faint Heart*. It was never written, but my mind was made up: that was what I would do and what I would become and that was what counted. What was Jeannie dreaming about that day? I could never guess about Jeannie. Too late to be a flapper, she was a positive girl, a decisive force. I asked her when she was safely married what she was thinking that day lying in the hammock, but she couldn't even remember 'that' day until I reminded her and she said: 'How do I know? They were the days when all I dreamed of was being presented at Court by Uncle Johnny (something in the Treasury in London). I suppose that's all I was dreaming of.'

In any case we were all on the verge of lighting lengthy fuses, although the explosion that would launch us would come much sooner than we thought.

But Jeannie's warnings of selfishness that day were ignored, because Tom's and Peggy's final indiscretion which brought the whole town into it, came at the Agriculture Show in which Peggy was a competitor in the Highland Dancing contests.

The Show was held every year in the permanent showgrounds, an area of about fifty acres. It was hard, dry ground and in the middle of it was an oval with a grandstand. It also had stables and empty spaces and it was entirely surrounded by a high corrugated-iron fence. There was enough ground, as a matter of fact, for two cricket pitches and a football ground. The perimeter and some of the open spaces inside were shaded by huge red gums, so old that every limb was stringy with ribbons of bark and dead wood and magpie nests.

The Show itself was primarily an agriculture competition for wheat, sheep, cattle, hens, butter, grapes, soft fruits, milks, flowers, sheepdogs. At that time (perhaps it is still the same) there was a tree-cutting contest in which pre-prepared thick trunks of gum trees were set up in the arena, and a plank slotted into them. The contestants hacked off the top of the trunk, standing on the plank. Sheepdog trials (mainly jumping), dressage, horse-jumping, trotting races, buck-jumping (rodeo) and district athletics were all going on at one time or another in the three days. But there were also visiting sideshows, bearded women and snake charmers, the whole family of fairground attractions. There were halls where local housewives competed anxiously with cakes, scones, breads, pies and full-course dinners.

Lockie MacGibbon had a boxing ring set up in a tent under one of the gum trees. He staged two kinds of contests at the Show. One was a wild series of elimination bouts for bantams, lightweights and light-heavyweights, though to what end the local boys were 'eliminated' nobody knew. The other kind of contest was a challenge by three of his own fighters to fight anybody for three rounds and stay on his feet. One of them was Finn MacCooil. A knockout in these bouts would count as a win and was worth twenty pounds of Lockie's money. Lockie also had other interests: a small zoo of animal freaks such as a tailless kangaroo and a Rhesus money with one arm and an embarrassed cocker-spaniel with three ears, and he also had an Aunt Sally for the impulsive pitchers and throwers who grew wild in our country, and one of the Sallies that had to be knocked down was an unmistakable portrait of my father.

Lockie had done it again.

Jack Turner, who ran it for Lockie, shouted to me: 'Come on, Kit, take a shot at your old man.'

'No thanks,' I said. 'I can take a shot at him any old time.'

Not far from Lockie's booth where the fighters crouched and jigged in their flat fighting boots and peignoirs there was another raised ring in the shade, but it was not for boxing. This one was a dancing platform, and all day we could hear the pipes of Jock MacDougall as he played laments, reels, and strathspeys for the Highland dancers. That squashed, curling, Chinese sound of the bagpipes can still cut open my mind when I hear it, because I am helplessly attached to the memory of this one summer's day. It is one of the best memories I have of Peggy MacGibbon.

At first I didn't see the dancing because it was a very busy time for a local reporter like myself. We dare not leave out anything, yet space was limited and we published only twice weekly. As technical training in concision it was excellent. I had to be at the Show almost at dawn, and since the trotting events were held in the evening I left it at dark, and I spent half the night simply sorting out my copy and learning elementary lessons in diplomacy – the diplomacy of who to ignore rather than who to put in, which is after all the real diplomacy.

Tom was a competitor. He was riding Fluke, one of Dolland the chemist's ponies, in the obstacle jumping (under 14 hands). He was a good show horseman, I think mainly because my father had always insisted on the long forward stirrup, English fashion, instead of the shorter and more backward position favoured by rougher-riding Australians. We had once owned two ponies, which Tom and I had ridden to school and all over the Billabong and deep into the bush. The ponies had been payment in lieu of cash by a farmer who had retained my father to sue a big sheep agent for breach of contract. My father had won the case, but the farmer had no cash to spare, so the ponies arrived and a year's supply of chaff. I suppose that particular mounted year was the happiest in my entire life, and Tom told me in 1940 when he could fly a plane that, next to flying, riding was the only time when he felt thoroughly, physically happy. The ponies had eventually gone to pay the butcher's bill, going the same way they had come in a curious retrogression to peasant trading in kind. But Tom had learned a great deal in that year, and when the Show was due plenty of local horse and pony owners wanted him up on their mounts, though not for dressage.

He won his small event and added one more little silver cup and blue ribbon to our store on the mantelpiece, and I saw him briefly in his cunningly patched jodhpurs (they were mine, lengthened, widened and restored by my mother) looking a little distraught because he was afraid that he had missed Peggy's dancing.

I went with him to the dancing platform and sat down on one of the planks set up as seats. There were two pipers standing by and about fifty spectators and about twenty young women and young girls and very young girls in full clan dress, tartans, bonnets, sporrans and soft, black, high-laced dancing shoes. They were waiting their turn to dance. The judges sat at a kitchen table near the dance floor.

'There she is,' I said wastefully.

Tom and Peggy had seen each other long before, but I was silkily impressed by Peggy MacGibbon in clan costume with greenish-purple tartan, plaid, velvet jacket, silk blouse and a bonnet with a long quill in it. She was a raving beauty and she knew it.

There was more than that.

We watched three small girls performing what Tom told me was a Strathspey. (Peggy had taught him enough in their dark evenings by the river. What else did they have to talk about?) The girls were pretty little Australian things but in the shade of our coolibah tree they were never a step nearer Caledonia than the hot day and the surroundings permitted.

When they finished I got up to go.

'I'm a bit too busy for this,' I told Tom. 'I can't wait.'

'That's all right,' he said absent-mindedly and he also got up and moved to a plank nearer the platform and as he did so I hesitated because I saw Peggy deliberately walk around to Tom and undo her diagonally-worn plaid and fold it, and then quite ceremoniously put it across his knees.

It was so publicly and so bravely and so boldly done that I looked at Peggy thereafter with a much more exposed nerve. She was flushed, she was serious, she was probably feeling reckless, but every one of the fifty townspeople watching, including her sister Smilie (also in tartan) and Mrs Craig Campbell and Peggy's friends knew what it meant, and I realized that there was probably some old clan blood in Peggy because the gesture was a profoundly tribal one.

Tom half stood up in amazement. Lovers look like lovers. No eyes could see, no tongue could talk, they were lost like polar explorers in vast white wastes. I think Tom had the athletic impulse again, because it seemed to me that his whole body bunched itself up as if he were going to lift Peggy up and carry her onto the platform and perform a raw Highland dance himself.

'Peggy!' Mrs Craig Campbell said sharply, calling her pupil to order.

Jock MacDougall (the town baker) was already in the corner of the platform squeezing and blowing and searching for his fluty, pipal note. Peggy walked up the steps, high-coloured, green-eyed and flying, although she was somewhat helped by the lace ruffles and tartan skirt and tartan socks and velvet jacket and the row of little silver buttons and her red head of hair.

The formal bow in a Scottish dance is as significant as a Moslem lowering his head to the east, it is barely perceptible yet extremely formal, as indeed the whole dance is because convention ties up every step as tight as a drum. But what someone like Peggy MacGibbon in love could do with it astounded me, and since she bowed publicly and deliberately towards Tom I felt everything that Tom himself felt.

The dance, as I made it my business to find out, was a Seann Truibhas, and though it lasted about five minutes it never developed more than eight or ten steps, repeated in multiple variations.

Peggy began with a curious little turn to the right, then she raised her arms in the bell-like shape of the Highland pose, and as Jock MacDougall squeezed a high-toned whistle from his pipes (the tune was 'Whistle ower the Lave') she began dancing that peculiar lifting, arched-toe, vibrating Scottish lilt with marvellous precision and a sort of succulent preoccupation, making a small circle, her crimson feet lifting, brushing, travelling – all correct technical descriptives for Peggy's devoted and quite purifying use of this highly vernacular dance.

There could be no doubt, even to a stranger, that Peggy was excelling herself. There were subtleties I obviously missed, but Peggy herself told me when I reminded her of Show day that she wept long salty tears half the night in the exhaustion and ecstasy of knowing what it was to live for an aerial moment outside oneself and outside all places of touch, taste, measurement and joy. Art was miraculously at work and everyone felt it, particularly the piper whose piping clasped Peggy like a physical partner.

I only once saw something comparable to it five years

later, during the war in Moscow, when Yermolaev (the world's greatest dancer, even including Nijinsky) and Lepeshinskaya were competing in a victory performance of *Don Quixote* with a bitter rivalry of dancing that went far beyond the borderlines of anything human; but that was another taste, another moment.

Peggy had simply been taken away somewhere by love, and I think we all wondered if she would ever come back to us. It was not easy, but she did bring her Seann Truibhas to the end with a reluctance, yet a precision which was perfect: a curious little turn, a small one leg up and one leg down step like a prancing horse and then suddenly it stopped and she stepped once to the right and to the left, stood still and bowed once more to Tom like a God bowing to another God. Who else were they but Gods?

As I have said before I do not breathe, I live by touch and by feeling and by sensing everything all the time, and I danced every step of the Seann Truibhas with Peggy, and for once I think Tom was taken aloft clean out of the normal air he lived in and he too must have felt what I had felt. There *is* art, because that is what art has always done to the onlooker.

My instinct was not to spoil it by remaining a moment longer, and I glanced at Tom who was simply standing up in his jodhpurs and waiting for Peggy to come down the steps. He was holding her plaid. I think people applauded almost in a panic of feeling, I don't honestly remember, because I got out of the way, although wherever I went thereafter I could hear the whirling and thin wailing of the pipes. I listened for them when they stopped, and was relieved again when they started.

12

All the gossiping town knew about them now, so it would only be a matter of time before Lockie and my father also knew.

But there is one question here that I must leave unresolved, because I don't know the answer, and can never find out now. I can only present the situation and try to reason it through, or make a guess. *At what point did Lockie MacGibbon find out?* that is the question. It may only be of psychological interest, but it may also have affected subsequent events. The incident that makes the question worth asking happened on the Saturday night after the Show.

There was always a 'stockman's night' on the Saturday after our Agricultural Show. This was a peculiar gathering, supposedly of all the stockmen and drovers and riders who came to town for the Show itself. It was always spontaneous and was held over the river on the Billabong in a stringy patch of bush which grew along a gentle stretch of the river. The stockmen came on their mounts from the Riverain sheep and cattle runs, small farmers came in their trucks, and townspeople on foot or by car or on bikes. Nobody needed to organize the gathering because it was really an instinctive Australian return to the bush. Many billy fires were lit and a dozen billies of tea were boiled, and you could walk around from one to the other along the river and drink, play cards, play two-up, sing ribald songs, or listen to our national ballads which most Australians knew by heart, or partly anyway.

It is not easy to explain the skinlike attachment Australians have to their ballads. I don't think anybody else has it in a popular sense except perhaps the Russians, but drovers and drapers and bar flies and boxers and preachers and schoolboys would all sit around the boiling billy and unashamedly declaim the popular verses of 'Our Andy's Gone with Cattle' or 'The Man from Snowy River'.

I reported this gathering for the *Standard* and commented on the fact that 'X', who was normally drunk in the gutters of Dunlap Street Saturday night, was on this Saturday upright under the gum trees which held the Australian nation together spouting lines from 'The Sick Stockman' or 'The Ballad of the Drover'. Old Mrs Royce, my employer, told me it was good, it was very good, it was too good in fact because everyone in the country would recite our national epics at the drop of a hat, but on the whole they were all ashamed of it so it was better not to antagonize them by making a public point of it. The town would only laugh uncomfortably at its own embarrassment, and that would spoil the 'stockman's nights' thereafter.

I heard, for instance, a fat farmer named 'Stubbles' Cox from Mindoon banging a tin mug on his boot and reciting drunkenly to its tinny tune:

> The Morning Star paled slowly, the Cross hung low
> to the Sea,
> And down the shadowy reaches the tide came
> swirling free . . .

That was all he knew but it was enough.

There were dozens of others, mainly the ballads of Henry Lawson who is the one poet of colonial Australia who has outlasted the rest, because he was born in a tent and grew into the shape of the country the way it was, and never derived anything from the English Lake Poets who influenced so many of his better-educated contemporaries now dead and forgotten. 'The Blue Mountain', 'The Roaring Days', 'Andy's Gone with Cattle' were Lawson's. I heard them all that night, and one other poet, Banjo Batterson, who had written one of our first great indigenous ballads 'The Man from Snowy River'.

Lockie MacGibbon seemed to know them all. Lockie was a good Australian and he was as near that night to what was a national theatre of the time as we would have. He was the man outside the tents of our country side-shows, and I could hear him barking at the top of his voice without any kind of expression:

> I rode through the Bush in the burning noon,
> Over the hills to my bride,
> The track was rough and the way was long,
> And Bannerman of the Dandenong,
> He rode along by my side . . .
>
> A day's march off my Beautiful dwelt
> By the tawny streams in the West;
> Lightly lilting a gay love-song
> Rode Bannerman of the Dandenong,
> With a blood-red rose on his breast.

Ten more verses told the story of how Bannerman swopped horses with the bridegroom when a bush fire caught up with them. The bridegroom escapes on Bannerman's good bay mare, and Bannerman is burned alive. And thereafter in the poet's dreams 'rides Bannerman of the Dandenong, with a blood-red rose on his breast'.

Lockie gave it no sentiment and he did not shift his voice an inch from his open-air bark, but it was Lockie that night who really put me on the crust of the earth I was brought up on. Lockie brought it nearer to me in his outside voice than I ever felt before or since. Australia was more Lockie's country than mine, though barely, but I felt what he felt: the same nerves tangled into the trees, the rivers, the plains, and our peculiar voice; and everybody else took it from Lockie exactly as he gave it and said: 'Good on you Lockie ...', the Australian accolade.

I suppose it was natural that Tom and I had a slightly different view of it as well. Tom and Dobey the Diver – the once-clever boy who remembered anything he ever looked at – were sitting on the other side of the river-bank reciting Victor J. Daley and Louis Lavater who hardly matter these days. But Tom knew the one other poet who mattered to us even more than Lawson or Alice Werner did. Twenty-five years ago Dorothea MacKellar had written a short poem called 'My Country', and for us it was the perfect division of feeling for the one country we had never seen which we called 'home' and the other one we actually lived in which *was* our home. The poem is an address by an Australian to an Englishman, comparing their roots, and though Tom was no expert, after listening to Lockie, he gave it enough meaning to have its effect on me until now:

> The love of field and coppice,
> Of green and shaded lanes,
> Of ordered woods and gardens
> Is running in your veins.
> Strong love of grey-blue distance,
> Brown streams and soft, dim skies –
> I know, but cannot share it,
> My love is otherwise.
>
> I love a sunburnt country,
> A land of sweeping plains,
> Of ragged mountain ranges,
> Of droughts and flooding rains,

> I love her far horizons,
> I love her jewel sea,
> Her beauty and her terror –
> The wide brown land for me!

That was Tom putting us squarely on the side of Lockie, though by a different route.

'Who was that?' someone asked in the darkness.

'Tom Quayle,' someone else said.

'Ah . . .' came the answer as if that explained it.

The poetry isn't the point I intended to make here. The real point is that Lockie MacGibbon found Tom in one of the dark little continents between the billy fires and the clanging (sometimes awful) recitations. He took Tom aside, and still using the unabated ringside voice he used for a responsive audience he said to Tom:

'Now here's a bloody young fool. Tom Quayle. Tom, I want to talk to you.'

Lockie was a little drunk, which was rare with him, and Tom told me that he instinctively looked around to see if Finn MacCooil was somewhere in the shadows. Lockie laughed at him.

'What are you worried about?' he said.

'Finn MacCooil on my back,' Tom said aggressively.

'But I've got nothing against you, Tom,' Lockie said, still addressing his side-show audience. 'It's your old man I've got it in for.'

Tom nodded. 'I know,' he said cautiously, wondering breathlessly if it was Peggy that Lockie wanted to talk to him about. Tom was about to leap defensively into the subject himself, but his Quayle instinct told him to wait.

'There's no reason why you and me should fight,' Lockie went on cheerfully as they went deeper into the bush. 'I don't believe in the sins of the fathers, do you?'

'No,' Tom said tentatively and stopped walking. He had gone far enough for safety.

'No?' Lockie confirmed. 'Then listen. What's the point in persecuting a hopeless case like me. You know what I am, don't you? I'm a showman, Tom, that's all. If I rub your old man up the wrong way you can hardly blame me, because he's such an interfering pommie bastard that someone has to take him down a peg or two or we couldn't even live in the same town with him. D'you see my point?'

'I'm not sure that I do,' Tom said non-committally. 'In any case he thinks exactly the same of you.'

'Does he? Well he's up the pole,' Lockie went on. 'I like everybody in this town and everybody likes me. Remember that, because most people hate your old man.'

Tom told me that he kept thinking: 'He's her father so shut up and don't say anything wrong and don't lose your temper. Just shut up, don't talk.' So Tom said nothing.

'Now take this court case, for instance,' Lockie said. 'It's all cock-eyed as far as I'm concerned.'

'But it's your case,' Tom blurted out. 'You started it.'

'I know. But I had to do it. Your old man forced me into it. They're cheating me, there's no doubt about it. Look, Tom, I don't beat my family, my girls are honest girls and go to Mass, and I love my wife. What's the matter with me? Nothing. I need the money, that's all, and I'm willing to close my eyes to a lot of things from here on if you just let me get safely through this case against that little bastard Dorman Walker.'

'Close your eyes to what?' Tom said, startled. Did he mean Peggy? Was he offering Peggy in exchange for victory in the county court?

'Everything! I can leave your old man alone, for instance. Never say a harsh word against him ever again. Think of that!' Lockie laughed heartily. 'And anything else you like.

You're the one who's been collecting all the evidence against me, you're the one who knows everything. Now give me a chance, Tom.'

Lockie was facing up to Tom with the aggressive show-manlike posture that never left him. The unseen crowd he was appealing to in this dark corner of the bush had no particular eyes and no particular body, and Tom had realized by now how alike Lockie and my father were, because Edward J. Quayle addressing the Great Judge and Lockie MacGibbon addressing the Great Crowd were single-minded enough to remove themselves entirely from the ordinary run of moral judgements.

'I can't do anything, Lockie,' Tom said stiffly.

'Why not?'

Tom shook his head.

'You mean it's against the law?' Lockie said to him incredulously. 'So what? The law isn't always right. You don't want to be scared of doing things your own way. You're an Australian, Tom, not like your old man.'

'It's not even that,' Tom said and knew he could never explain himself to Lockie.

'Religion?' Lockie suggested.

Tom shook his head again and tried to say nothing, to keep quiet.

'Scruples? Principles?' Lockie concluded hopefully, unresentfully.

Tom, I must repeat, was not quite eighteen. Physically he was a sort of joyful kangaroo, morally he was an atom, but he was not going to open up any of his code books to Lockie. Scruples were already good allies to have, but principles suggested only a part of him because he was still making them up from various sources. But he already had strict values for himself, and they were comparatively simple ones.

'I can't do anything for you,' Tom said stubbornly.

'All right, Tom,' Lockie said good-naturedly. 'But I think you're going to be sorry. You as much as your old man.'

That suggested Peggy again, but Tom could not believe it. Lockie was too good a father, too proud of his family and his daughters to bargain Peggy for the toleration of an enemy. Yet what else could it mean? Curiously enough Tom himself never thought of what he would gain or lose of Peggy in the deal. Both he and Peggy were far beyond such touchable corruptions.

Lockie went off cheerfully, unbothered, undefeated.

'Never mind, Tom,' he said. 'I'll win the case anyway.'

He had not begged Tom for anything, he had only tried to make a legitimate deal. But he left a nagging little mystery for us because even Peggy never knew if her father had already found out about Tom. Although if he didn't know then he certainly knew soon enough afterwards.

*

The effect that Peggy and Tom's public behaviour now had on the town did not amount to anything much at first, in fact it became a joke because the situation promised to develop into something as good as any of the visiting dramas we could see in the Shire Hall or in the sideshow tents that came to the country towns. (I remember running home, aged nine, after seeing *Uncle Tom's Cabin* performed in a circus tent lit by acetylene lamps, scared white because Simon Legree had beaten the daylights out of little Topsy on the stage.)

But there was also resentment, because on Monday we woke up and all the oranges from my father's twenty carefully nurtured trees had been picked and each one stuck on the pointed tip of the corrugations of our tin fence. We had an excellent garden, not only oranges, but peaches, grapes, passion fruit, nectarines; and my mother's English roses and English violets in season would catch the south wind and flavour the whole town. The last time the victims were my mother's roses, and this time it was my father's oranges.

'Vandals!' my father moaned when he saw it. He was knotted with hate. A year's hard and rewarding work was spiked on the fence. 'Convicts!' he cried at the town. 'Gallows' meat.'

'But why did they do it now?' my mother said.

'MacGibbon and his henchmen,' my father said, as if he were clamping Lockie between his furious jaws.

I knew it wasn't Lockie, it wasn't Lockie's style, and anyway he wouldn't go so far. It was obviously Finn Mac-Cooil, probably a little drunk. Hearing about Tom and Peggy, he was paying the first instalment of many savage reprisals yet to come.

Tom agreed. 'It was Finn, all right,' he said. 'No doubt about it.'

It was definitely Finn's style; no home for Finn, no safety, no heart that wanted his heart.

'Did Finn ever have any yearn for Peggy MacGibbon?' I asked Tom.

'Finn? No. At least I don't think he did.'

'Ask Peggy,' I suggested.

We met again that morning at the station where Tom and Peggy, pursuing their public policy, stood together saying good-bye to Mrs Craig Campbell on the platform. Now that Peggy had made her bold tribal gesture of love I wanted to see how it worked. Peggy was obviously Tom's senior in behaviour, and his protector as well. But in his threadbare khaki pants and thin shirt and uncontaminated look Tom was not yet aware of what was looking after him. He had fallen gratefully into their exposure with satisfied relief: no more deception ...

'Hello Peggy,' I said to her. 'When do you begin teaching?'

Peggy had easily won her class championships and now she would qualify as a professional dancing teacher because she would be eighteen in a few days.

'Next week,' Peggy said. 'Why, Kit? Do you want to learn?' she teased.

'No,' I sighed. 'But you ought to teach Tom. He'd be very good at it.'

She laughed and pushed her arm through Tom's and I flinched for all the ovular eyes that saw them and all the lips that judged them. I looked quickly for a diversion for them.

'Did you know that Ravel had just died?' I said to Tom.

'No!' Tom said in surprise.

Ravel meant 'Bolero' in those days, but he also meant the Pavane and the Noble and Sentimental Waltzes and Le Tombeau.

'What a pity,' Tom said regretfully. 'No more pavanes.'

Peggy looked at me and then at Tom, and for the first time (she said afterwards) she suddenly understood and liked our whole family, something I had long ago felt for her own family, mainly because I admired her mother but also because I liked Lockie.

The train pulled out then, so we three were left on the station together.

The afternoon would be a public holiday to make up for the three heavy days of the Show, so Tom and Peggy made an appointment to meet at the swimming hole and then Tom came with me up the sandy street by the bank towards the back door of the *Standard*.

'I told Peggy about the oranges,' he said, 'and you were right. She thinks it was Finn MacCooil. She says he was jealous.'

'So he did have his hopeful eyes on Peggy,' I said.

'I suppose so. But it never occurred to me, Kit, because Finn is such a lost sort of soul.'

'Poor old Finn,' I said.

'Finn's all right,' Tom said grudgingly, 'as long as he doesn't do anything really stupid.'

We crossed the road near Dorman Walker's feed and grain store and Tom was thoughtfully whistling to himself the Ravel pavane we liked – a sad simple almost hesitant dance for some dead Spanish child he had seen.

If Tom had known it he was anticipating a pavane of our own for that day, because in the afternoon we finally entered the arena of local tragedy, and it knocked hard at our safe little world and transformed every one of us into something entirely different – particularly Tom.

13

Peggy never liked to remember that afternoon, but I did convince her to recollect one thing. I wanted to know how she imagined they were going to survive all the fuss and trouble – inevitable when both families knew what was happening and reacted the way we knew they would.

'I didn't care about that,' she said. 'I was so in love with Tom that I wasn't afraid of anything.'

'You were overdoing it,' I pointed out.

'No, I wasn't. Tom was miserable with all the subterfuges, so I did everything for him. He couldn't come out in the open because he was protecting me. But I could.'

'But they never would have let you get away with it,' I insisted.

Peggy thought about it a moment and said: 'We might have, if it hadn't been for that afternoon.'

I doubt if this was so, but there is no way of judging or even guessing about alternatives like that. There is, in fact, no other proven path but the one we take.

When Tom and I went down to the swimming hole after lunch there were already about ten other youths there, diving in a hole a little farther down the river where one of the old river boats (not MacCooil's) had been wrecked thirty years before and was now lying ten feet under. For years we had ransacked the old boat of everything we could bring up, and though there was little left that we could get out of her now, we would still dive the ten feet by leaping off the high bank and then try to penetrate the under-decks a little further. It was dangerous, but it was so frightening when you were in that dark labyrinth of narrow passages underwater that we all knew when to stop.

Dobey and Tom were working out some arrangement of going into the hold together, but I had outgrown the sport years before. I had a swim and sat on the bank, wet and cool and warm and dry, looking at our dry landscape, at the weeping willow trees dragging their wet hair in the river higher up, at our low colonial houses, at the gum trees along the Billabong. There is something about the way an Australian gum tree hangs that is difficult to convey and I was looking at one of the very old trees that grew in a little bend of the river and trying to think up some definite idea of its character. The only word that comes to my mind now is 'drip-dry'.

A light touch of someone's knee on my back woke me up.

'What are you dreaming of, Kit?' someone said.

I lifted my head and looked upside down at Peggy Mac-Gibbon. It was pleasant to be touched by Peggy, it was flattering to be taken into an intimacy which Peggy was trying to wrap around us all. Maybe she could have overcome the family feud.

'Sit down, Peg, and watch these idiots,' I said.

She sat down next to me in her cotton dress, under which she wore her swimming suit. She had a towel over her neck, a bathing cap hung on one thumb. She watched Tom and Dobey going over the high bank arms locked together as they hit the water, and we waited a long time for them to come up. But Peggy, like my mother, had learned to trust Tom's ability to survive anything and to emerge from anything at the right time. He came up, we knew he would, but there was something in Tom's physical self-confidence and certainty which also made women feel close to him and safe.

'When did you come?' Tom shouted when he saw her.

'Hours ago,' she said. She already sounded like an affectionate wife. 'Go on with your sport.'

But Tom and Dobey came out of the water and sat down near us, leaning back on their hands and drying themselves in the sun. Dobey was a lanky, knobbly youth, and his plaster-cast was chipped and written on and grimy, and Peggy said it was a disgrace. 'You ought to be ashamed of yourself,' she said to Dobey.

Dobey blushed. He, who knew *Morte d'Arthur* by heart and could tell us all the known elements, would say nothing. He was a silent boy and he was beginning to remind me more and more of the gum tree that hung itself over the bend in the river. A drip-dry boy, a drip-dry country we lived in.

We sat still without talking for some time, soaked by our buzzing air and simply drifting through one moment without thought that there was another. It was pleasant. Then I saw Grace Gould coming down one of the dirt paths from the railway line, and reluctantly I broke the circle of silent fire we had given ourselves and met Grace in the tomato plantation which a grocer named 'Tum-tum' Ryan had planted on the slopes.

I had made a terrible mistake with Grace. I rarely acted on impulse, but I had given her one written page to read which I needed somebody in the world to see at some time or other before I died, and at twenty death is often frighteningly near; I was sometimes convinced I was going to die the next day. The luck just wouldn't hold, the sun would simply go out.

'I read it,' she said to me and fumbled in a canvas bag she carried.

'No! Keep it,' I said quickly. 'I don't want it here.'

'I didn't know that you could write like that,' she said to me and looked at me quizzically as if there was hope, there was possibility, maybe there was even something to gamble on here. I had watched two middle-aged people in the town falling in love and I had written eighteen lines demonstrating that late love was possible. Maybe the leaf was falling but that was not necessarily the end. I remember every undaunted line of the eighteen:

> Some love is liken
> To the oaken leaf:
> Autumnal, beautiful,
> Until old twinge of frost
> Is cruel to its little truth
> And there it dies of beauty.
>
> Blest then upon the air,
> It loves its grace:
> Pausing, momentous,
> It must decline.
> Not torn to earth,
> But fallen there in multitudes.
>
> Yet life perpetuates.
> There's an act of stillness –
> Seasonal, various,
> Then tender furies
> Shake the world
> And the child is born.

I did not ask Grace whether she understood it or not, or whether she liked it or not, I didn't want comment. She had in fact answered me, and I was instantly in retreat, regretting my silly gesture. Her calm, almost bland and waiting face was willing, but I wasn't, not yet anyway. But Grace was clever enough and generous enough to leave it alone.

She pointed to Peggy who had taken off her print dress and was walking towards Dog Island where we usually swam.

'What a marvellous figure Peggy's got,' she said, 'except for the legs.'

'What's the matter with her legs?' I asked.

'Dancer's legs,' Grace replied. 'The muscles will bulge awfully in a year or two.'

'Do you think so?'

'Inevitable,' Grace said happily.

I looked at Peggy's legs. I don't remember what part of the female body we depended on then for our erotic hopes. It certainly wasn't the bosom that selected the best part of our desire. I think it was the whole person. Grace was right. Peggy had a perfect Venusian figure, but that was Tom's business not mine and I did not even think about it.

There was no trouble among any of us that afternoon until the usual business with Dog Island suddenly began. Peggy and Tom were sitting on the edge of the little island dangling their feet in the river and nobody bothered them: there was an unwritten regulation among us to let lovers alone.

I was lying on my back near Grace when I heard one of the Philby twins shout, 'Look out, Tom,' and I turned over and sat up in time to see Finn MacCooil, who had crept up to the Island behind Tom. Nobody had seen him arrive. Before Tom could do anything, Finn put his foot on Tom's back and pushed him in.

I laughed. Tom had been caught.

But Peggy was furious. She leapt up, and with a clenched fist she swung wildly at Finn MacCooil and caught him on the side of the head. It must have stung. Finn got a grip on Peggy's wrists, but Peggy broke free and began to swing wildly, a few of her dozen fists cracking Finn's lowered head. Finn was shouting at her to stop it, but he suddenly lost his temper and pushed Peggy off the island, not gently but rather savagely.

I knew what was about to happen and stood up.

Tom was out of the water on to the island, and he had Finn around the ankles and they began to wrestle on the now slippery surface.

'Where are you, Mickey?' Finn shouted.

Mickey Murphy was another pugilist from the neighbouring town of Nooah. He was a bantam with a broken nose and rather flat feet and he leapt into the sport by getting a grip on Tom's neck and bending him back and forcing him into the water.

Peggy, the fighter, was already back on the island grappling with Finn who shouted: 'Get off me, Peggy. Get away.' Then he simply threw her off.

I was already on the way down because this was no ordinary sport. Both Tom and Finn were now in a violent temper with each other over Peggy, and Peggy's intervention had ensured a conflict which would obviously become very violent if it weren't stopped quickly.

'Tom !' I shouted as I ran. 'Give it up. Get away from it.'

But Tom, his face red, was on the island again and now fists were flying. Even before I got there Dobey the Diver was also there trying to separate Tom and Finn and Mickey Murphy, but the slippery little knob of dirt made any kind of restraint unpredictable and Tom, though down, pulled at the nearest legs and over went Murphy with Dobey clinging to him.

'Stop it! Stop it!' Peggy was now shouting.

They ignored her, and when I reached the island and climbed up to try to do something Mickey came up on the other side and butted me with his head and I went down.

Not everybody thought the way Peggy and Dobey and I

did. The Philby twins (our side) were ready at all times for a good rough and tumble, and all the boys who had been diving into the wrecked river boat saw the scrap, shouted to each other, and suddenly appeared. They split into the two groups it always came to – Protestants and Catholics, because Tom and Finn were both popular and this was an inevitable division for the suppressed violence of our suppressed differences.

Perhaps only Dobey and I in that tangle knew what was really happening. In the middle of it Tom and Finn MacCooil were fighting a real fight, and the viciousness soon affected everybody and now twenty youths were shouting and scrapping a little more seriously than they had intended. And though I was still trying to stop it, even I was infected.

By now I was more off the island than on it, but Tom wasn't and I could see Tom's arms flying and his head and knees and elbows in action with the rest of his body. Peggy had been shouting out to him. 'Tom. Get out of it. Stop. Please stop!'

'Keep out of the way, Peg,' Tom shouted desperately. 'Don't come near.'

Peggy would have gone back into the battle, but I was in the water and I pulled her away and said breathlessly to her: 'It's too late, Peg. Just keep out of it . . .'

I didn't finish. A flying figure landed on my shoulders and I sank six feet under. When I came up there were more bodies flying through the air, and the water was more slashed with legs and arms and bodies than seemed sensible, even to the fracas. Only about six people could really fit on that slippery island, and with youths trying to get up, being pulled back, getting up, being thrown off, the weight of flesh in the air or hitting the surface of the water was thunderous. I got up once, was pushed, slipped and hit my head and slid on my back into the water, and even before I came up someone landed on top of me. The area was small, the human ammunition was concentrated.

Then blood began to appear. I saw Dobey take an awful fall on the island and then go into the water. He was handicapped by his arm in plaster, and when he came up he shook his head as if he were a little dazed. I lost sight of him because I was still trying to get up and pull four people off Tom who was fighting like a wild animal and thus provoking more violence because anyone who came anywhere near him was knocked silly, so Tom was a fair target. I wanted to get him out.

I don't know how long it lasted, too long, because I only remember, after a long time, Peggy screaming at the top of her voice as she 'trod' water:

'Where's Dobey. Tom! Tom! Where's Dobey.'

I didn't take any notice at first, but when I came up after another heavy plunge someone near me said, 'Where is he?'

'Dobey's gone,' Peggy was crying.

'Stop it,' I shouted now.

At first nobody took any notice, but I heard Mike Murphy shout to Finn: 'Dobey's gone, Finn. Stop it, for Christ's sake.'

Everybody stopped immediately.

'He must have gone out,' Finn said looking around at the bank.

'He didn't,' Peggy cried.

Now we began to say where we had seen him. I had seen him dazed, someone else had landed on top of him, he thought. Someone else had seen him briefly afterwards. Someone else had felt something underwater. There could be little doubt: Dobey had been knocked out, gone under, and had failed to come up.

We all began to dive at the same time, and it was not like

the situation we were in with Fyfe Angus. It only took five minutes, and one of the Philby twins found Dobey and brought him up. He was blue and swollen, his lips were puffed out, his body lifeless.

We dragged him to the bank and Finn began to use the Schaeffer resuscitation method we knew, pushing on his back to get the water out of the lungs. Finn pressed, lifted, pressed, lifted. The rest of us stood around in a large crowd, nobody tried to push anybody back, and we didn't talk.

Finn was bleeding from the nose and his blood dripped unpleasantly on Dobey's back, so Tom pushed him aside and began to press and lift, press and lift. We took it in turns and kept it up. Someone had run up to the nearest house to call the ambulance. We kept up the resuscitation until we saw the box-backed ambulance arrive at the top of the little hill.

It was Tom who was pressing and lifting at the time, and when he heard someone say 'There's the ambulance', he suddenly sat back on his heels and looked up at Peggy and shook his head and said what nobody else had wanted to say.

'It's no use, Peg. We were too late.'

Suddenly the nerveless skin of Dobey's high-diving body revealed the truth, as if once the words were said the visual evidence became apparent. The most grotesquely living thing about Dobey was his dirty plaster-cast. The rest of Dobey was lankily and calmly dead.

'Don't stop!' Peggy cried to Tom.

But Tom shook his head. He was kneeling beside Dobey; his hands were no longer on Dobey's back but on his own knees. We stared at Tom.

It was Finn who cracked the tense little surface. Finn had always had more simple faith and trust in Dobey than he ever gave to anybody else in the town; perhaps we all did;

but Finn groaned aloud and I suppose he secretly wept. What he also did was to lean over, and with a terrible blow at the kneeling Tom knocked Tom sideways over Dobey's body.

'You can take some of that, you bastard,' Finn said as he delivered the blow. 'You did it.'

Tom half straightened up, but he kept on his knees, bending over Dobey. He was too upset to resist. He kept his head down and kept his hands on his knees and waited like a man awaiting an execution. But Peggy was white-faced with anger and she said savagely to Finn:

'I'll kill you, Finn, if you touch him again. Leave him alone.'

Tom was like a man with a broken back, we all were. In an instant the crowd pulled away, no longer anxious to look at Dobey. The ambulance men had arrived after running straight through 'Tum-tum' Ryan's tomato fields so that their boots looked bloody. They knelt, they touched, they looked, and when we asked as if we still needed proof whether it was true, they said:

'How for God's sake, did it happen when you were all here?'

'It was Quayle and that lot,' Finn snarled again.

'You started it, Finn,' someone said.

'But you did it,' Finn repeated between his teeth, giving his little hissing sound. 'You did it,' he went on repeating almost to himself as we watched them wrap Dobey in a blanket and carry him up through the tomatoes to the ambulance.

14

It was natural that Finn should blame Tom, because the division of enemies in those contests had always been so simple. Being a Catholic, Dobey was logically on Finn's side, being a Protestant Tom was on the other side. But Tom and Dobey were good friends, and even in this fracas there had obviously been no animosity between them. On the contrary Tom's admiration for Dobey was as deep as Finn's desperate kind of affection for him.

Nonetheless, for those who were not there to see the incident it was easy to believe in a day's clumsy rumour that Tom had somehow been responsible. That is how the town heard about it anyway. They also added the sauce of Tom and Peggy's situation, and the scandalous twists and the commentaries of shame made a moral mess of both of them. Their original sin was somehow the cause of the whole tragedy.

There was a dangerous pause, though, while the physical situation was cleared up. There was a quick inquest. The pathologist said that Dobey had been unconscious and had been asphyxiated while unconscious – drowned while senseless. The situation was argued out in the basement of the police station. Everybody talked, nobody was blamed, nobody dared blame, the whole thing was declared an accident because no other verdict was possible. Nobody had mentioned love or religion, but that was the issue which was left standing as the issue. Dobey was allowed to die in peace, but the rest of us remained with the unresolved problem of village bigotry.

When I saw Tom in the afternoon he said he was going to see the Dobeys to explain what had happened, because the air was foul with all the evils of misconception.

'I'll go with you, if you like,' I offered.

'All right,' he said glumly.

We crossed the town and knocked at the back door of the little three-roomed wooden box where the milkman and Mrs Dobey lived. They had always looked older than their age. Mr Dobey was a diabetic and Mrs Dobey was a rather sad, flabby woman.

'Mrs Dobey,' Tom said nervously when she came to the door. 'I just came to explain about Dobey, I mean Jack, and say I'm sorry ...'

'What do you want to explain?' Mrs Dobey said listlessly. 'I don't know why you came here.'

'But I just want you to know that I wasn't fighting Dobey, I had nothing against him, we all liked him, it really wasn't my fault ...'

'Go away,' Mrs Dobey said to Tom. 'Why do you come here?'

'To explain,' Tom said desperately.

'Dobey was really trying to stop the trouble,' I said to Mrs Dobey. 'He was only trying to help, and nobody would hurt him deliberately, Mrs Dobey.'

'Go away,' Mrs Dobey said and closed the door.

We left, there was nothing else we could do.

Tom was in misery, and there was a dangerously poised silence and a no-talking situation at home because my father now knew everything about Tom and Peggy and my mother too, but they at least held off until Tom could recover from the blows he was taking now.

Dobey was buried on the Thursday and I went with Tom

to the Catholic Church to attend the service, but at the door we were turned away, not by the Fathers who knew nothing of what was happening, but by Finn and Lockie who were acting as ushers. Lockie looked as if he would kill Tom.

'If you ever come near Peggy again, I'll beat the daylights out of you,' Lockie said. 'I'll break your arms and your legs.'

'Listen, Lockie . . .' Tom began.

'Shut up!' Lockie hissed because the service was about to begin.

'But . . .'

'You're not wanted here,' Finn said pugilistically.

The two boys looked at each other, knowing that everything between them would have to be settled somehow, and the only way either understood it now was violently. I knew how it would end, sooner or later.

Tom refused to be put off and we went to the cemetery and waited there until the cortege arrived. Then we joined the group around the grave and Tom and Peggy looked helplessly at each other over the chasm of that gash in our universe. They had already come through a great deal of opposition – their own internal opposition as well as so much that was outside, and as I listened to the priest and saw Peggy's white freckled face flooded with her golden tears I knew that she and Tom would never surmount this one. They were far too young.

All the boys were there, everybody suddenly felt what we had lost, it was a genuinely regretful day. When it was over I watched Peggy and I could see that she was constraining herself from going to Tom who had taken such a beating. His unprotected eyes must have been eating into Peggy's heart like acid into the flesh of a bird.

But something had happened to her. Peggy looked once

and walked on with her mother. Lockie stood like a little eagle beside them, watching Tom and almost holding Finn like a thunderbolt in his fist, ready to launch it at Tom's head if he approached.

As we walked out of the cemetery I could hear the slugging sound of the earth as spadeful by spadeful Dobey was covered with our farms and our vines and our fruits and our gardens and our rivers and our trees and the awfulness of our realization that upright was now down, that Dobey the broken bird had finally come to earth.

*

I suppose if it hadn't been for my mother and Jeannie, my father would have made his moral lesson for Tom straightaway, and made the furious attack on him which eventually came with sulphur and hell. But the women, holding him back, gave Tom enough time to survive. At seventeen death is a dangerous lesson to learn, because it can frighten you out of life for ever. Tom was fighting a battle for his life in those few days, and maybe if Peggy had been there it wouldn't have been so brutal, but Peggy was cut off now for ever. Tom ate, Tom possibly slept, Tom went to work and sat in the cubby hole; Tom walked, Tom talked, and Tom lived in his air; and in some ways I felt more of what he felt than he did himself, because I could touch it and he couldn't.

He tried once more to talk to the Dobeys but they sent him away, and that was probably the scar that would never heal for him, because in a very short space of time Dobey the milkman and diabetic died the way his old horse had died a year before, he lay down and didn't get up, and Mrs Dobey became a curiously deranged lump – meeting the local good women (who came down to her house to help her) at the door with nothing on from the waist up and being polite and normal but half-pure and half-naked. She finally refused to wear any clothes at all, talking awful sin and awful retribution. She tried to purify her soul by burning her flesh on the kitchen stove until one day she overdid it and scorched her whole body so deeply that she never recovered. That was two years later: but the scar was already on Tom's back long before it happened.

I think what shocked him out of it was being attacked by Finn one night as he spoke to Peggy. The incident was violent and brutal and led to an even more violent and brutal situation.

We were sitting out on the front verandah brooding when I heard someone call softly. 'Tom!' I knew who it was, and Tom leapt up and ran outside, down the path. I should not have followed, but I couldn't help it.

They did not fall into each other's arms but stood a little apart, almost shyly as if they were now too precious to risk with childish exercises.

'I can't stay,' Peggy said. 'I wanted to see you . . .'

'I'm all right,' Tom said.

'Don't listen to what they're saying about Dobey. Don't worry about it.'

'It wasn't my fault, Peggy,' Tom said. 'It simply wasn't my fault. I didn't even see Dobey . . .'

'I know. I told everybody. I told Lockie. I told them all.'

'Lockie will kill you if he knows you've been here,' Tom said anxiously.

'He said he'd cut off all my hair if ever I saw you again. But I don't care any more.'

'Then for God's sake go home before they miss you,' Tom said.

'I don't care . . .'

'Please go, Peg. Don't come here.'

'I'm all right,' she said. 'I wanted to see you . . .'

That was all, because Finn MacCooil came out of the corners of the world and leapt on Tom. There was a brief brutal fight and Lockie was suddenly there and I pulled Tom away and a passer-by, Paul Simpson, intervened as well, and Peggy was taken away crying at her father: 'Leave me alone. *Just leave me alone!*' Tom was suddenly limp and then suddenly like a tiger and was at Finn MacCooil almost with his teeth but we held them apart, and Finn said that if he wanted to be beaten to death to come the next night at seven o'clock to Charlie Castle's garage and they would fight it out properly.

'All right,' Tom snarled. 'All right. All right ...' His teeth spoke, not his tongue or his throat.

My father had come to the front door and shouted out: 'What's going on?'

'Nothing!' I said and took Tom quickly down the road and kept going beyond the slaughter yards to the old aboriginal burial ground where some cactuses grew. We sat on the mounds in the darkness for a while and then Tom said: 'I'm all right, Kit. Don't worry,' and we walked back again and I knew that this time my father would be waiting.

Our dining-room had in it a long and handsome mahogany table which was pitted with scars caused by the men who had assembled our house (it had been shifted from another town with its furniture) using it to straighten bent nails on. The fifty years of habit, which being a Victorian father made important, meant that if my father was sitting at the dining-room table working, instead of at his roll-top desk, there was going to be terrible trouble, as if he needed all his flanks wide open and no other responsibilities anywhere around him. My mother and Jeannie had gone to bed, and that was also a bad look-out for Tom.

'Sit down!' my father told him.

My father knew all the psychological legal tricks: a man

seated was easier to suppress than a man on his feet. Tom sat down.

'Kit,' he ordered me: 'Go to bed.'

I sat down. 'No, I was in this too,' I said with unusual bravado, 'so you might as well deal with me at the same time.'

'As you wish,' my father said coldly. 'But the real issue here is the girl and that's nothing to do with you.'

Tom said nothing.

My father had been suppressing a powerful engine of temper, and now he slowly let it have its way as he began to attack Tom: 'Do you know that the whole town thinks you were responsible for that boy's death?'

'Let them think it,' Tom said with a shrug. 'It's not true.'

'True?' my father said, snatching the word out of the vicious Australian air. 'Who cares in this town about truth? Who cares, I say? What counts in this country is the appearance not the reality, the shadow never the substance...'

'*I* don't care,' Tom said stubbornly.

'But I *care*!' my father shouted. 'I have to care. How dare you get mixed up with that girl...'

'I didn't get mixed up with her.'

'Don't lie. You did! And behind my back. Do you know what *collusion* is...'

'Oh, that's ridiculous,' Tom said.

'Don't say that to me,' my father shouted. 'In a town like this what other interpretation would people put on your association with her except some sort of collusion to evade the law, to play a dirty game. Already that little wretch Dorman Walker has been at me...'

The point had just reached me. My father was frightened that Peggy and Tom, working up a relationship, would actually be interpreted as an attempt to fix up some shady deal between appellant and defendant which would influence or circumvent the law, or whatever sickening phrase they gave it.

'But that's silly,' I said. 'Everybody thinks that Tom and Peggy are a weird joke, that's all.'

'Keep out of it! You don't know the law, but Tom does.'

'What law?' Tom said bitterly. 'What crass idiot would ever think that Peggy and I could cook up some sort of collusion to outwit the law?'

'Everybody would think it!' my father cried. 'You want to tarnish this family's whole reputation. You want to jeopardize the way we have lived, your sense of honour ...'

'*There is no honour!*' Tom shouted back. 'What honour are you talking about ...'

They went on quarrelling at the tops of their voices, bitterly and without any kind of sense, because there was no sense left in either of them. Lockie had threatened to cut off Peggy's hair if she ever saw Tom again, but my father was not able to invent something so frightening although he threatened Tom with expulsion from the family, an end to his career, and some sort of tragedy which would affect the whole family.

'All you're thinking of,' Tom cried furiously, 'is your legal purity.'

'And what else is there to think about?' my father bellowed, red-faced.

Lockie thought of violence, and my father thought of a lawfully pure reputation. I knew that it was hopeless trying to see sense or trying to restrain either side now.

'If you see that girl again,' my father said heavily, 'I swear that I will leave this town. You know what that means, don't you, to your family and to me. You know what difficulties we have already. I swear to you, I tell you, that I will tear us up from this town and leave it, if you ever talk to that girl again. Do you hear ...'

Tom heard, and my mother standing in her dressing-gown at the dining-room door was like the ghost we longed to haunt us.

'The neighbours will hear you. You're shouting,' she said miserably to my father. But she was helpless and she knew it.

'Let them hear,' my father cried. 'They know everything anyway. Let them hear some truth for a change,' he bellowed towards the window as if the township was waiting outside and hanging evilly on every secret word we said.

15

The bloody battle between Tom and Finn was only another preliminary to the final bout between Lockie and my father. In other circumstances Finn and Tom might eventually have become accustomed to each other as they grew older; a few years later they might even have adapted themselves to each other's failings and got on well. But part of the conflict had been built into them almost from the day of their birth, and if duelling or gladiatorial combat had been the practice in 1937 only death could have satisfied them.

Instead of the pistols, they beat each other unmercifully but skilfully with boxing-gloves – the respectable and prehensile remnants of the duel.

In St Helen we had a garagist named Charlie Castle. Like Lockie, and often with Lockie's help, Charlie promoted minor contests in the ring. Charlie had the ring. He was the local agent for the Willys-Knight car, which he considered to be the best car in the world, and he planned to prove it by driving a four-seater around the showgrounds during one of the shows, zooming up a specially constructed ramp and turning a complete somersault with the car, which would be weighted at the back with bags of sand. He eventually tried his somersault, which became known as 'Charlie Castle's Leap', and it killed him.

Charlie kept all his new-model Willys-Knights out of his glass-fronted garage so that he could keep his boxing-ring in it. Charlie did not box himself but lived day and night in a greasy blue boiler suit. Charlie had no flesh, only a dirty boiler suit. Sometimes in his roped-in boxing-ring, which you could see through the very dirty windows of his garage, we would watch drunken ex-pugilists from the city who were in the town begging for work as grape-pickers. They would shadow-box in memory of the good old days.

Occasionally genuine blood feuds were settled at Charlie Castle's, and though clear victory by knock-out was desirable it was very rare. So Charlie Castle's decision as referee was considered a fair alternative.

Nobody needed to say much in the town about Tom and Finn, because by the next night the whole town obviously knew, and when Tom and I arrived at the garage at seven o'clock we couldn't even get near it. The space inside the dirty windows was full and the street outside was overflowing. Our Roman holiday was in session.

'Good on you, Tom,' someone shouted loudly when we were seen. 'You'll do!'

'They'll soon be carrying the little bastard out,' others suggested.

The comments were normal according to the normal division. Tom was well liked, so was Finn.

We tried but we knew we would never get through the crowd so I said to Tom: 'We'd better knock at the front door of Charlie's house and go in that way.'

'Vultures!' Tom said savagely at the crowd.

'Calm down,' I told him sharply. 'Temper's not going to do you any good here.'

'Ahhh!' he said disgustedly.

We were let in by Mrs Castle, whom we always expected to see in a boiler suit like Charlie's but she was a tiny little woman who simply said: 'Charlie's in the kitchen,' and we followed her down the dark passage.

Charlie and Finn and Mick Murphy were sitting in the

kitchen in which everything was covered with oilcloth, including the chairs. Probably it was the only way to cope with Charlie's permanent skin of grease. The three of them were drinking beer.

'Hello, Tom. Hello, Kit,' Charlie said. 'Sit down.'

'No thanks,' Tom said boorishly.

I sat down and pointed to a chair for Tom, and Mrs Castle asked us if we wanted a cup of tea. I said 'Yes, please,' and we sat grimly silent sipping rival tea and beer as if even the liquids of the world were divided between us. We heard a lot of shouting outside because the audience was getting impatient, so Charlie looked at his pocket watch and said: 'Yes, it's time,' and we followed him into the back of the garage where Tom and Finn stripped and got into shorts on the black and greasy floor of the workshop among the broken arms and legs of old Willys-Knight automobiles and we then went out into the garage proper which had a dirt floor, and so did the ring.

Two lights over the ring blacked out the rest of the surroundings, and the classical accoutrements were all there – bucket, stool, sponge; everything but the gloves.

'Where are they?' Mickey said angrily to Charlie.

'I thought you would bring a set,' Charlie said to Finn.

'What for?' Finn said. 'You ought to have them.'

'Just a minute,' Charlie said and went over to a greasy cupboard and came back with four gloves.

We all stood in the middle of the ring looking at them as the crowd shouted restlessly for us to get on with it. Two of the gloves were regulation and perfect, one of the other pair was also perfect but the right hand glove of this second pair was small, hard, and stained yellow.

'Do you want to use this set?' Charlie said. 'Or shall I send over to Lockie's place for another lot?'

'No,' Tom said impatiently. 'These'll do.'

'Then you'd better toss for the gloves,' Charlie said and Mickey tossed a penny. Tom called and won the toss and made the choice.

That was a mistake. There may have been something of aesthetic vanity in Tom's choice because instead of choosing the odd pair he chose the perfect pair, and later on he would regret it.

'All right, gentlemen,' Charlie said with all the old-world courtesy attached to this traditional bloodletting, 'Your gloves on, please.'

I tied Tom's gloves on his square fists and square strong fingers. I glanced at his face once. It was not the usual brick-brown-red, but pale and weightless, and those limpid blue eyes looked more vulnerable now than I had ever seen them. Only his mouth was set like a piece of hot iron.

'Gentlemen,' Charlie called again and we all went to the centre of the ring. 'This will be a contest of six rounds of four minutes each. I want no holding, no chinning or elbowing, no butts, no biting or bearding. You will break clean when I tell you and you will go to a neutral corner if I tell you to do so. A knock-out is an outright win, otherwise my decision is final. Do you agree?'

We mumbled like men mumbling responses to Divine Offices.

'Then shake hands, go to your corners, and when you come back you come back fighting and may the best man win.'

Tom and Finn exchanged that double-fisted form of love which begins these contests and I pulled the stool out of the ring. I had seen Mickey, Finn's second, giving him lengthy advice at the last moment. Weren't they both professionals? I had no professional advice to give Tom since he already knew more than I did. All I could give him was a little psychological propaganda.

'You're as good as Finn,' I said, 'but you've got something Finn hasn't got. You're not going to win with temper, Tom, or by being right. Only this,' I said and I tapped my head.

Tom ignored me. He was too highly pitched to comprehend, and my hope was that Finn was just as nervously reckless and savage as Tom was. Charlie clanged his bell, and Tom turned and faced the professional-looking Finn who, up till now, had said almost nothing, but I heard in the sudden stillness the faint little hiss he gave – that warning of an impending execution.

It began badly. Finn clinched the moment they met and Tom told me afterwards that Finn said in his ear, digging his hard chin into the little hole in Tom's neck where it joined the shoulder: 'You watch your balls, Quayle, because the first chance I get I'm going to dig my knees in deep,' and he lifted a knee and jabbed Tom in the groin.

'*Foul!*'

There was such an outcry that, though I hadn't seen it myself, I had seen Tom flinch painfully and I rushed into the ring and got a grip on Charlie's shirt and shouted above the whistling and booing: 'Are you going to let that go on?'

Charlie had already separated them and he said to Finn: 'Now listen, Finn. You're a better fighter than that. If you try any of that Showground stuff here I'll make sure that you never fight again anywhere. Now behave.'

Charlie had been holding them apart, literally, with one hand on each of them. I glanced at Finn and felt terribly sorry for him, because I knew that he had kneed Tom despite himself. Finn would have succumbed to despair years ago if he hadn't given himself a substitute for all the advantages he didn't have. I had always believed that his dirty tricks went against his deeper desires, but Finn had to level himself up to Tom and Tom's secure world, somehow, or rather pluck Tom down from his safe, untrammelled life, and this was his only way of doing it. I didn't resent it, and I don't think Tom did underneath all the other furies he felt. Finn didn't use a dirty trick thereafter.

But when Charlie let them go, almost before Charlie got out of the way, Tom swung a vicious punch at Finn's head which was so quick that it could also be considered a foul under the circumstances. Finn took it sideways and looked stunned for a second before he could recover.

'Foul!' the word rang out again.

But this time Charlie let it go, and thus began the brutal display of temper which they were both too far gone to control. There was no order and discipline in what they did, not at first anyway, and they fought stupidly, wildly, blindly and bloodily because both had soft noses and were bleeding by the end of the first round.

Both of them were breathing so heavily and were dealing out such reckless punishment to each other that I doubted if they would last the six rounds.

'You're mad,' I said to Tom angrily as he sat down at the stool. 'If you keep your head you'll have a chance, but otherwise ...'

I wiped the blood off his shoulder and face and tried to reach him by reason, but Tom's eyes were saturated with disregard for himself and for anything else, and he told me later that it was all the noise and shouting that had made him feel sick as well as furious at the outset. To be a bloody spectacle was the very thing he was then forming his whole life against.

'Use your head,' I said helplessly as he got up for round two.

They began again the same childishly wild flaying of air and of each other, and I could hear Mickey Murphy shouting to Finn: 'Hold him off and use your right, Finn. Hold him off.'

They couldn't hold each other off, but I noticed now that every time that odd little right-hand glove hit Tom anywhere it shook him. It was obviously like being hit with a fistful of cement.

'Time!' Charlie shouted.

Tom hung his head and breathed deeply as I poured water from the sponge over him. There were no gum guards to protect the teeth, and I looked at Tom's cut lip to see if his teeth were all right, but he shook me away.

'It's that right glove,' he said, breathing heavily. 'It's just like being hit with a horseshoe.'

'Then calm down and keep out of the way of it.'

'Too late now,' Tom said grimly, as if the whole mould of the fight had been cast already.

The third round began to change the shape and pace of the fight, because the professional in Finn was slowly emerging from the temper. Finn was only eighteen but he had already been fighting in professional bouts for a year, and some of them were vicious and clever bouts against better fighters than himself. He had more obvious skill, more rhythm, more understanding of what it was all about, technically; and once he began to use skill instead of simply scrapping, he had all the advantages. Curiously enough his telephonic hissing stopped. Additionally, too, he had a fistful of iron in his odd right-hand glove.

Round Three was clearly a turning point, and time and time again Finn stood off, or rather kept Tom off with a long left, and simply clubbed Tom with his hard little right, and Tom took every blow like a battleship being bombed. He was backing up most of the time now and he was glad to hear the bell and so was I. When he came to the corner I said to him nervously: '*Now* do you see what I mean? Finn's using his head.'

'It's that right glove,' Tom said stubbornly.

'Maybe it is. But he's not scrapping any more, he's fighting intelligently.'

Tom was still too blind to see it. His temper was longer because his anger was far more sophisticated. Too many things were being fought out here, and Tom knew and understood more than Finn, who was so far fighting a single issue which covered everything.

It was clear in Round Four that Tom would lose. Finn had developed such a professional sway, a heel-and-toe rhythm, such an easy-flowing of the shoulders that Tom looked clumsy and heavy in the same ring with him. Tom began to cover up more often as blow after blow was carefully placed. He was more and more afraid of Finn's right, so he ducked and twisted and swung, and Finn hit him hard on the face and the chest and the kidneys with that god-given glove on his right hand.

'You're going to lose,' I told Tom desperately and angrily when he came out of Round Four. 'Your only hope is to watch him and outwit him.'

'He's better than I am, Kit,' Tom said dispassionately.

'No, he's not,' I snarled angrily, not even trying to put conviction into my lie.

'I should have chosen that glove,' Tom said wearily as he stood up for Round Five.

'Forget the glove,' I said. 'Just keep away from it.'

Round Five was all Finn's. He boxed Tom cleverly, and although Finn was visibly tiring, Tom was visibly being beaten up blow after blow, and though some of Tom's own short lefts and wide-swung rights reached home, the sheer quantity of punishment was telling on him, and Finn knew it.

I said nothing between Round Five and Six. Charlie would only have one decision to give, and Round Six was clearly Finn's. In fact Finn was dodging and prancing, cornering

Tom in the obvious hope that he would knock Tom out, but though Tom was badly cut up and his face and his lip, nose, and left ear were bleeding (Finn's nose also) he was determinedly indestructible. Just before the bell that ended the last round, Finn caught Tom under the left shoulder with his iron right, and Tom staggered and went down but was up again immediately just as the bell went that ended the contest.

Charlie Castle came to the centre of the ring and said: 'Before I give my verdict are you both satisfied?'

Tom stood there stubbornly, his gloved hands at his side and he said: 'No. Let it go on to the finish.'

Charlie looked at Tom who was quite calm but more like an executioner himself now, and Charlie said: 'Are you quite sure, Tom?'

'Yes.'

'Finn? You want my decision, or you want to go on?'

'I'll go on as long as he will,' Finn said.

'All right! Four more rounds.'

'No,' Tom said grimly. 'I said to the finish.'

'Finn?'

There was a moment's silence and the audience now began shouting, 'Let them finish it, Charlie. Let them fight it out.'

'All right, all right,' Finn said angrily. 'What's he want me to do: cut him into little bits?'

Tom looked at Finn without anger or fury, and Charlie said to me and to Mickey Murphy: 'Do you two agree?'

Mickey hesitated, but I suddenly knew now that Tom would win so I said quickly: 'Yes, Charlie. Let them get on with it.'

'All right,' Charlie said and the audience roared its approval.

I had no doubt now. I think I knew Tom would win when

I saw that all his visible anger had gone. Tom knew that he would never give in, he also knew now that he could take all the punishment that Finn could give him; he knew what I didn't know which was that Finn's blows were getting weaker; he also knew that he was recovering rapidly himself.

'Back to your corners,' Charlie shouted again above the noise. 'I'll give you an extra minute break now, but when you come out come out fighting.'

Tom sat down on the stool and I could see that he had relaxed. 'Now use your head,' I said like a battered old expert. 'For Christ's sake.'

'Don't worry,' Tom said. 'Finn's not going to beat me. He can't.'

Perhaps Tom knew then what I only realized later on. They came out fighting, and once again Finn boxed Tom cleverly and well and his right was punishing Tom, but Tom had, after all, learned to use his fists in the same school as Finn, and now Tom watched and waited and retreated and used the ropes the way Finn used them (Tom had never fought in a proper ring before), and though Finn again punished him unmercifully, or so it seemed, Tom was not so broken this time as he had been before.

At first I thought it was just superior physique. Tom's abstinence and his hard internal purity were a better basis for survival than Finn's cheerful drinking and early womanizing. Tom only had to stay on his feet long enough and he would wear Finn down.

Round Eight was, in fact, the second turning point. Tom was a good dancer and had an internal sense of physical ecstasy, and he too was beginning to flow into his punches rather than extract them from his body like rotten teeth. Boxing is all rhythm; fighting is half-rhythm and half chopping wood. Tom had stopped chopping wood and now, blow by blow, he was hitting a tiring Finn, even though it was Finn who was attacking and Tom who was back-pedalling; but his blows on Finn were more powerfully and more effectively useful than Finn's iron right hand had ever been.

The round was Tom's for those who had watched closely. When he sat on the stool he leaned his head back and stared at the ceiling and simply went somewhere without me, not caring about me or about Finn or about anything except the one point left to this – outlasting everything. But I realized then that he had what Finn didn't have – an utter conviction in himself and in his necessity to survive and outlast and outlive and emerge and crush, whereas Finn had been born to lose this fight. I think Finn had somehow, in some secret recesses of his childishly-smashed heart, pinned some curious hope for himself on Peggy, as if she represented his last hope of emerging from an early and continuing disaster which had turned him rotten even before he had ever had a chance to be whole. But it was Tom who had the prize, and Tom knew it and Finn knew it. Finn had nothing, Tom had everything and would never give it up. If he did he would have lost the intrinsic nerve that he lived on and sucked life from.

Poor Finn. I felt everything he felt, but Finn did not understand his tragedy whereas I did.

Round Nine was the obvious switch, because now Finn was retreating and Tom was stalking him, and as it became clear to everybody what was happening they all shouted and screamed at Tom to finish Finn off.

'Finish him!' a whole claque began to shout with every one of Tom's hard blows.

Suddenly Tom, who was crowding Finn onto the ropes and hitting him on the head, stopped and dropped his hands and turned around with a distorted face and shouted at the top of his voice to the unseen audience: 'Shut up, you bastards!'

They shut up and Finn, too tired for his soul to recover or even to understand what was happening to him, simply held up his arms and danced like a robot as Tom hit him over the body and the head until even I could see the flesh on Finn's body shaking with Tom's hard and powerful blows.

In two more rounds it became worse and worse for Finn and at the end of the second one Tom was fresher than he had seemed all evening. 'I wish Charlie would stop it,' he said miserably as he sat still and let me swab the blood off his neck and arms.

'Don't let Finn fox you,' I said nervously. 'He can recover.'

'No. He's done for,' Tom said.

Round Twelve was the end. Finn's head was loose on his shoulders, his breathing was too heavy, and he had been coughing terribly between the rounds, and when he came out and made a great pretence of being lively and fit Tom simply repeated Finn's early tactic: he held him off with his left and hit Finn with a shoulder-driven right across the side of the head, then another one under the arm, to the kidneys, and a left to the shoulder, the arm, and with methodical persistence under the arm again and the side of the head, the kidneys, the chest, and finally the diaphragm, and Finn sagged to his knees, the sweat pouring off his unhappy and unrescued face. He began coughing and couldn't get up and Charlie ordered Tom to a neutral corner and began counting, watch in hand.

Finn got up, but Tom didn't even move.

Finn simply stood in the middle of the ring in what was now a silent auditorium, coughing and waiting for some final blow from life which would crush him and kill him.

Tom never delivered it. He simply stood in the corner untying one of his gloves with his teeth. He got it off, unleased the other one, dropped them where he stood and then walked across the ring and got through the ropes and left, almost running.

Finn didn't even notice what had happened. He turned around helplessly for a moment to see where he was, and then he held his chest and began coughing awfully again, and Mickey and Charlie helped him down. He was, in fact, unconscious on his feet. The physical fight in Finn was also intact, but the spirit had been executed.

Tom knew what he had done, or rather what had happened. He had not really beaten Finn at all. Finn had simply been outlasted by a morality which nurtured the family but not the strays. One small boy in our town could not be rescued by our social heart because we didn't really have one, except in charity which is death. The gods were therefore laughing because they had cleverly used one innocent man, Tom, to bring about the ruin of another innocent man, Finn, who would end up in the gutters of our town like his father.

After the fight Tom would not go home. It was nine o'clock at night, but he went down to the river and stripped off and went in and washed himself, as if he needed a whole river to wash away the effects of that fight. He put his clothes on over his wet body and we walked silently through 'Tum-Tum' Ryan's tomatoes. We were just walking up the path to our house, deafened by the frogs and crickets of the Billabong, when I heard a wild cry from behind us.

'Tom!'

Peggy leapt into his arms and Tom was too tired to do much but just hold her head and wait. She looked up at his face. It was a mess, and she pushed her fist into her mouth when she saw it.

'Lockie'll kill you,' Tom said to her wearily. 'Go home, Peg.'

'Oh no ...' Peggy said, touching his smashed-up face.

She didn't ask who had won or what had happened; they were the farthest thoughts from her thoughts. Tom pushed her gently away and said, 'Go home, Peg, for God's sake. You'll be in terrible trouble ...'

She nodded like an obedient child, her face still stricken – not only for Tom's face but for their situation now, because she had been locked up in her bedroom that night and she had crawled out of the window and must now get back undetected. We didn't know about it then, but we knew later on because by mid-day the next day the whole town knew that Lockie MacGibbon had caught Peggy coming back and had cut off all her hair, and I thanked our pagan stars that my father hadn't seen Tom and Peggy in that brief message of time, because he would surely have ripped us up from that town and wrecked us, just as surely as Lockie seemed to be wrecking the family he loved so much.

16

Bitterness is worse than anger because it is anger that has settled down to something deeper, calmer, and more painfully deliberate. The situation between our families had been worsened by shock so that now it was very bitter, yet I still half expected Lockie to call off his litigation against Dorman Walker (which meant my father) and I half expected my father to do something to stop the final ferment seething. But I was young then and touched harshly by everything touchable, and I didn't realize that neither Lockie nor my father could call back their lives. There is no machine to stop a man's will, nor is there one to interfere with his wanton destruction of himself and his neighbours.

In our own family there was an awesome situation of strain and silence and waiting. But at least my mother had used her powerful and quite untapped feminine threat to censor my father. My mother had wept silently when she saw Tom's face, not only for the face but for the pain of the event and for the misery of our absurd predicament. Tom simply became sullen and brooding and curiously obedient, going to my father's office and working there as if all was normal inside his seven deep skins. We all knew it was not normal, if only because Peggy MacGibbon was invisible and in shorn exile.

I don't remember anything of the next three weeks except that the politics of the world were just beginning to affect us all seriously. Austria was being prepared for the anschluss, and there were violent demonstrations in England to demand arms for the legal government of Spain. Chamberlain had also said that Hitler's threat to Czechoslovakia, that little country on the eastern borders of Europe, was nothing to do with Britain.

I remember these things well because I was watching Tom closely and he had not been going down to Hans Dreiser's. But I saw Dreiser once a week when I went to report the activities of a newly-founded local Arts and Sciences Society, of which old Hans was a natural supporter, bringing along with him a volume of Goethe to read if asked. Hans gave me the political weeklies and monthlies for Tom to read, all marked heavily in red pencil on the important issues, which I suppose was also part of my own early education although I didn't know it then. Tom read, Tom could still feel other agonies beside his own. Barcelona had been bombed by the Germans, and though bombing of the defenceless is common-place now it was a tragedy then.

Lockie's court case came to sessions towards the end of February, and though some of the town's interest in the bitter rivalry had waned, there was enough left to make it impossible to get into the gallery of the court unless you knew someone there who could arrange it.

Our local County Court was just behind one of the pubs (The Sunshine) and in the middle of the day the smell of stale baked beer saturated the old wooden walls, and I think this foul smell of the Australian devil and Lockie MacGibbon was the perfect atmosphere to keep my father attuned to his responsibilities.

Yet the case itself was dull, except for the way it ended.

Litigation in an Australian court is much the same as it is in an English court except that the methods are second-hand. In Australia, behaving like a gentleman in the well of the court is not quite the same as behaving like a gentleman in the back street courts of old England. My father, far from restraining himself in the English manner, was perfectly willing to let himself go in the Australian way, and his asides and professional instructions to the judge (Mr Masters G. L., 'an Australian political back-room barrack-room lawyer' my father called him: a combination of evils hard to match) were often insultingly so superior that I marvelled at the patience of Justice Masters sitting in the little legal pulpit above us and listening. But it was well known that Judge Masters always took a big nip before sitting in the same court where my father was working, so his usual attitude was resignation: a sigh, a weary glance, then he might say heavily to my father: 'Oh very well, the point can stand.'

My father's first tactic in the case was the good legal tactic of using the law rather than the issue, hoping to get out of the whole thing. I think only in law could my father subjugate his moral ferocity to common sense, or rather he could at least make the gesture. He argued at first that Dorman Walker had no case to answer because he was, in fact, only the agent for the Univermag Fire Insurance Company, and since the petition was directed personally at Dorman Walker and not at the real principals, the case was in fact misdirected unless the learned counsel for the plaintiff wanted to make it a case of tort.

'Tort?' Judge Masters said in astonishment. 'Explain yourself, Mr Quayle.'

'Myself?' my father said drily, 'or the law?'

'Just your particular interpretation of our law,' Masters said, trying to alienate my father into a little English ghetto.

'*Our* law,' my father pointed out, 'is by origin the Common Law of England.' Tort, my father pointed out, was a breach of a general duty which obliges a person to refrain from injuring his neighbour, as distinct from a breach of contract which is simply a duty owed to a contracting party.

'Well?' the Court demanded.

'My client is not, strictly speaking, the contracting party and there's been no breach, therefore the only alternative I can think of, in the learned counsel's mind, is that he is accusing us of negligence, or something like that which comes under the legal heading of tort . . .'

'Ridiculous,' J. C. Strapp said.

My father was not going to let a good mocking argument go so easily. He wore an alpaca coat buttoned up with three buttons, his face was hot and as usual tight with a ferocious jest at the expense of something Australian that sat up there, or down here.

'Well, I had to assume that my learned Australian friend knew the law, and I can't imagine him trying to sue my client for breach of contract, since the contract is not even with him.' My father was in fact trying to force Lockie to tackle the monster (the Univermag Insurance Company) rather than the flea (Dorman Walker).

'Who signed the contract?' the judge asked.

'My client signed the contract, but that does not make him the principal.'

'The issue,' J. C. Strapp said, 'is not who is the principal, but who signed an agreement promising to pay up on a Fire Insurance policy, and that policy was signed by Mr Dorman Walker sitting there.'

There was an argument about corporation law (responsibility above the individual) and a dozen other issues, and I must say that my father had them all against the wall, including the judge who began to show signs of predictable temper with my father's method of arguing.

Finally the Judge stopped it by rapping his pencil on the wooden pulpit. 'I would like to remind counsel,' he said to my father, 'that this is not the State or the Federal High Court. It is only an intermediate court. Counsel's arguments are too sophisticated for our humble efforts here, so if he wants to argue the issue in his own sophisticated way, he can do that in more elevated circumstances than this court. Here he will have to argue the case as presented. It will go on. I find that your client has a case to answer, so please proceed accordingly.'

My father simply raised his hands in resignation as if a dog had just passed judgement on a lion. 'Oh, very well,' he said petulantly.

There were more legal arguments that do not matter now. What mattered in that courtroom, through all the legal coruscation, was my father's intention now to prove that Lockie MacGibbon had fired his own house to collect the insurance money, and the more the situation progressed in that direction the happier my father became, and the more worried Lockie MacGibbon looked because he had never seen my father doing what he was best at. Even the formulations of the language, which Lockie thought he used as English, had become particularly tangled with my father's legal vocabulary. Lockie did not like it, and I think he realized very quickly that he had made a mistake.

My father called all the evidence he and Tom had collected: the affidavits, the firemen, the Seventh Day milk collector, the analysis of the bathtub. He put each man in the witness box, not chronologically, and though J. C. Strapp could have questioned them all if he wished he only asked them a few unimportant questions each, so that all the visible evidence pointed to the obvious fact that (a) Lockie had returned to St Helen that night, (b) there had been petrol in the tin bathtub which had been set alight, and (c) Lockie had, on the evidence, conspired to compound a felony, namely burning down his own house for the insurance money.

It was only on the second day that Lockie himself came to the stand, put there by his own counsel who so far had allowed all of my father's evidence to stand unchallenged, which rather foxed all of us. Now, Lockie was asked by J. C. Strapp who was a fat, pudgy, effeminate man with a left-handed gesture of grandiose emphasis and a good lawyer whom my father respected:

'Will you tell the court, Mr MacGibbon, whether at any time, either Mr Dorman Walker or counsel representing him here ever asked you, personally, if you had come back to this town on the night of the fire?'

'No, they didn't ask me,' Lockie said.

'Did you, in fact, come back to the town that night, Mr MacGibbon?'

'Yes, of course I did . . .'

There was a great deal of astonished laughter in the courtroom because that was not only a surprising admission, it was obviously a clever one. Everyone knew that Lockie had always claimed, by inference if not directly, that he had never been near his house that night.

The judge had been ordering silence and Strapp went on:

'So that all this evidence of your movements that night, which emerged like a plot of evil from the previous witnesses, would easily have been obtained honestly from you if they had simply asked you a simple question?'

'Yes.'

'Which they failed to do?'

'Yes.'

'Good on you, Lockie!' someone shouted loudly and there was laughter all around us and J. C. Strapp smiled goodnaturedly.

'Well then,' Strapp continued. 'Let us turn to all those complicated affidavits and all this evidence of that incriminating tin bathtub which has been so famous in our town, and which, incidentally, was deliberately stolen . . .'

'Objection,' my father said.

'Oh, all right,' Strapp said indulgently before Judge Masters could comment. 'I withdraw. We can generously let pass how they got it, it's too petty. All we want here, Mr MacGibbon, is an answer to the question that all this mysterious analysis has supposedly answered for us, as if once more we were trying to hide something when in fact we are not.'

'Mr Strapp . . .' Judge Masters began.

'I'm sorry, Your Honour, but the question I was leading up to is this: Did you, or did you not, put petrol in that tin bathtub, Mr MacGibbon; I mean at the time relevant to these events, or thereabouts?'

'No,' Lockie said.

'Are you quite sure?'

'I swear,' Lockie said vehemently.

'Do you know if anybody else put petrol in that tin bathtub, I mean at the material time of these events.'

'Yes.'

'Who was it, Mr MacGibbon?'

'My wife . . .'

Another uproar, and I watched my father. He was quite calm. I would say that he was happy, even though all his carefully constructed case against Lockie was being knocked to pieces, and I guessed that, in fact, win or lose my father was only really happy in the well of a court where in the wits of counsels of law the moral issues of right and wrong were argued out with no interference from amateurs and outsiders, and strictly according to one of the codas he loved so much.

'And what, Mr MacGibbon,' Strapp said from his belly when the noise had subsided, 'did your wife put petrol in the tin bathtub for?'

'To clean some suits of mine,' Lockie said. 'She soaked them . . .'

Half the court began to cheer, and the judge knocked his hammer on the wall behind him because it made more noise than the little pulpit where he kept his notebook, and he shouted: 'I shall have order.' The court police were tapping people on the shoulders, and in the pause I caught up with my laggard shorthand, sitting at the reporters' table with a spinster from a newspaper in the neighbouring town of Nooah.

'Cleaning suits . . .' Strapp repeated lavishly.

It was a good argument, because in those days most of our suits were cleaned that way. Petrol was not dyed and there were no dry-cleaning shops, or rather one had just been opened in the town but it was far too expensive, so wives used either petrol or ammonia.

'I shall, of course, ask our friend the Head of our Fire Brigade, "Muscles" (pleasant laughter), I mean Mr Murray Smith, the next question I am about to ask you, Mr Mac-Gibbon, which is this: What do you think would happen to a bathtub full of dirty petrol, from which of course the clothes had been taken and which had been left in the tub so that all the dirt could settle to the bottom, what would happen to it if a fire started elsewhere in the house and the house caught fire? Do you think that the petrol in that tin bathtub would obligingly remain unlit, or would it burst into flames with a whooooosssh?'

'It would burst into flames with a whooossh,' Lockie said.

More delighted roars of laughter and Strapp gestured like a Roman senator acknowledging a friendly acclamation, and he turned to my father and said: 'I think Mr MacGibbon will gladly answer any questions my learned friend would now like to put to him.'

My father stood up and pushed his glasses up on his nose and said to Lockie, 'Remember you are under oath to God,

150

your God and mine, so answer the questions with that in mind ...'

Lockie blushed, which I hardly expected him to do, but it was the blush of a blow received and another one that would be given some day in retaliation.

'When you came back to St Helen,' my father said, 'I mean the night of the fire, what brought you back in such a hurry through the night.'

'I had to bring back one of my fighters, Finn MacCooil, who had to go with Charlie Castle to another match next day, and you can ask Charlie if you don't believe me ...'

The court was delighted again.

My father was calmer than Lockie, though, and I think this bothered Lockie and it also bothered me the wrong way, because I felt that my father had something else up his sleeve, or rather he was searching for something else that he knew existed. I looked at Tom to get a clue, but Tom was watching as intently as I was from his seat at the table near my father.

'Did you go to your house that night – at any time?'

'You mean inside it?'

'Yes, or into the grounds of your property?'

'No, I did not.'

My father looked puzzled, whether it was a trick to look puzzled or not I don't know, but I think he believed Lockie. I certainly did and so did Tom, and I remember too that Peggy had already told Tom some time ago that Lockie had not returned to the house that night.

'Did any of your pugilists go there that night?'

'Not that I know of.'

'One last question, MacGibbon ...'

'Your Honour!' Lockie shouted furiously. 'Can he call me MacGibbon like that ...'

'Mister Quayle,' Judge Masters said, obviously checking

his own temper. 'There is no need to bring your personal feelings into this courtroom . . .'

My father swung around on Mr Justice Masters like a lion snarling at a jackal. 'I strongly object to that sort of intervention from the bench on the grounds that it is bringing an attitude and a suggestion of vicious inuendo on my professional behaviour. You, sir, have no right to suggest any such attitude on my part, unless you yourself are bringing in outside matters and attitudes which you know of, and which are irrelevant here. If the bench does not retract, I will ask for this case to be stopped on the grounds of prejudice and . . .'

'Oh, all right. *All right*, Mr Quayle. *All right!* the Judge almost shouted, white with rage and perhaps tinged with fear too, because I knew now who was dominating this courtroom. 'I merely wanted to suggest that in this country, Mr Quayle, the word Mister is a valuable asset to a man's name, and a courtesy always due in this court to a plaintiff. I forgot your English manner, Mr Quayle, and withdraw my hasty remarks . . .'

My father neither thanked him nor acknowledged any apology but turned to Lockie who was now visibly terrified of this rival bantam who fought everything and everybody in a milieu that Lockie did not even understand.

'May I ask, *Mister* MacGibbon,' my father said in brutally sweet reasonableness, 'who was the person in your family who first discovered the fire?'

'My daughter Peggy,' Lockie said slowly.

At the mention of Peggy's name Tom looked quickly at my father, and for a moment there was so much secret violence between three men in that court – my father, Lockie and Tom – that I felt the hairs at the back of my neck rise and fall and rise again.

'I see,' my father said slowly.

152

He took off his glasses, put them carefully into their case and when he closed it with a snap the whole court jumped in astonishment. He looked thoughtfully at Tom, as if weighing something up, he looked at Lockie, and he said to the judge: 'I think that is all, Your Honour. Oh, except that tomorrow, since I think it is almost time for this court to recess for the day, tomorrow I would like Miss Peggy Mac-Gibbon, whose full name I believe her father will give us, I would like Miss MacGibbon to be called to the stand as witness to events, and I would like an order to that effect.'

'Peggy is too sick to come here,' Lockie suddenly shouted like a man who was protecting his last untarnished joy in life.

There was an argument. My father was sweet, cold reasonableness, and legal too. Had a doctor been called? How old was she? Eighteen now. It went on. My father said he would wait, indefinitely, so the court would also have to wait! but he insisted on the witness being called eventually and it was agreed that, if Peggy were well enough, she would come at ten o'clock the following day.

*

I don't really know what my father thought would happen with Peggy, but like Tom with Finn MacCooil there was an air of certainty in him which made me feel that he was sure of his victory anyway. He was too calm. Like Tom in similar circumstances the anger had gone out of him, and yet there was something so savage and sure in him that I knew instinctively that Lockie had already lost. How he was to lose was another matter. I asked Tom that night what he thought, but Tom was obviously, for the first time in his life, trying not to think. The air he breathed had deserted him, and he wanted nothing real, nothing as down-to-earth as anticipating a terrible scene in the morning – which was

Peggy faced with my indestructible father. So Tom simply waited as if everything else in his life was now in suspense.

The next morning we were all in court at ten when the recess ended, and my father was going through some legal rigmarole with Dorman Walker in the box when Lockie and Mrs MacGibbon arrived with Peggy, and my father hesitated in the middle of a question and allowed the buzz of interest to continue and he waited, without turning around to see what it was because he knew, for Peggy to be shown to the bench where the witnesses sat. She sat next to her father and Mrs MacGibbon was given a seat in the gallery.

My eyes, with my touchy brain, leapt from Tom to Peggy, from Peggy to Tom, and perhaps everybody in the court did the same thing, except my father who kept his back turned to it all and remained undivided.

Peggy was a brave sight. She wore a green silk kerchief over her shorn head, and the first and rather silly question in my mind was: how the devil had Lockie done it? Surely Mrs MacGibbon had not known. Definitely not, I decided. We all knew that Peggy's hair had gone, and that changed the recognition of the face and of Peggy, who had lately been very beautiful in my dry eyes, and was now an even more remarkably assembled human being. She and Tom simply looked at each other, and Peggy bit her lip once and showed no other sign of pain or care, and then as if by agreement they did not stare at each other any more.

'If we might continue,' my father said.

It shook the whole court. He still hadn't turned around.

'Mr Walker,' my father went on. 'Would you say, in your long experience as a fire insurance agent, that fires are ever spontaneous?'

'No.'

'Something always starts them?'

'Of course.'

My father went on with a series of pointed but apparently worthless questions before he turned around and saw Peggy; but he still did not call Peggy to the stand. He called the Fire Chief, 'Muscles' Smith, and he put the same questions to Muscles and then got almost deliberately tangled up in a point of law with Strapp and the Judge – both of whom objected, but my father knew he could carry it off anyway.

I guessed by now what he was doing. He was letting the atmosphere of the court soak into Peggy. He was not being histrionic, as Strapp was inclined to be, but he gave a thoroughgoing display of a man who knew more of what he was doing in this court than anybody else, and I saw with Peggy's wide green eyes that here was somebody who had to be feared like a vengeful devil.

He finally got around to Peggy, almost casually, and Peggy sat down behind the little barrier and nervously tightened the scarf around her head and looked at my father as if there was no one else in the room. I think she was looking to see what kind of a man he really was, and what he would do to her. I know now what had really happened between herself and her father, but to tell it at this point would be to upset the continuity of what I am doing. But Peggy's white, freckled face and red eyebrows and green eyes were all soaked with some long stain of misery, and my father looked at her carefully and put on his glasses, and if he saw what I saw it must have affected him. Maybe it did, it is hard to say in the light of what developed.

'Peggy,' my father began, but neither gently nor ungently. He was in his own forum and life here was not the same as it was outside and therefore life had to be measured on the terms of the moment, none other. 'Peggy,' he said. 'I am sorry we had to bring you here, but this, strictly speaking, is not my desire . . .'

'Mr Quayle! . . .' Judge Masters warned angrily.

My father looked up at the Judge and was so drained of temper and fury and so obviously unvicious that the Judge did not pursue it.

'I want to ask you some questions, Peggy, but before I do so I would like you to realize that what you say may seriously affect the future of your father . . .'

'Objection!' cried Strapp angrily. He, like everybody else in the court, was poised nervously, wondering what my father was up to.

'Why, Mr Strapp?' my father said. 'Do you want me to ask this young girl questions without warning her of the consequences? Do you want me to launch into unpleasant subjects without warning her first what it might mean to her father?'

I had the curious feeling that he was persuading Peggy, by a psychological trick, that her father was almost on trial here, and what followed convinced me of it.

'May I continue, Your Honour?' my father said.

'Continue, Mr Quayle, but watch your step please.'

'Of course,' my father said calmly. 'Now, Peggy, I have to make sure that you understand what is at stake so that you don't make a mistake which may damage your father . . .'

'Mr Quayle . . .'

'I must insist that I warn the girl,' my father said to Judge Masters, 'even if the court doesn't think it necessary.'

'Very well, but . . .'

My father turned back to Peggy and I think he looked at her scarf, at her invisible and lost head of hair. 'Now, Peggy,' he said gently. 'Do you love your father?'

Peggy bit her lip then and looked at her father and looked at Tom and said: 'Yes, I do.'

'You wouldn't want to see anyone hurt him or see him maimed or put in prison . . .'

'Objection!' shouted Strapp in a real temper.

'I allow it, and I warn you, Mr Quayle, you are on the borderline of treating this court with malicious disrespect.'

'Well I don't insist,' my father said, but he looked at Peggy in such a way that she was asked the question silently again.

'No, I don't want to see him hurt or put in prison,' she said unhappily, her head down, mumbling as if the admission was proudly given but given with difficulty and pain. In any case it was clear in Peggy's mind now that her father was, in fact, on trial here, and I know from Peggy herself that the only person in that court who had a grip on her now was my father.

'Good,' my father said, 'because your truthful answers to my questions may actually help your father . . .'

'Objection,' Strapp shouted. 'I am counsel for Mr Mac-Gibbon.'

'Mr Quayle!' Judge Masters said wearily.

'I withdraw the comment,' my father said, 'and apologize.'

'Now Peggy,' he went on. 'I believe you are an honest girl . . .'

I glanced at Tom and he was rigid with concern and Peggy stole a glance at him as if to ask him what was happening, and what could he do about it.

'Yes.'

'You believe in God, and God's retribution, don't you?'

'Yes, I do . . .'

'Mr Quayle, I am beginning to lose my patience with you,' Judge Masters said grimly. 'Will you please come to the point so that this girl can be relieved of what is obviously a painful duty.'

My father looked up at Judge Masters once, and even I

writhed in distaste for that look. It was almost as if he had called the judge an unlicensed idiot.

'Very well, I'll make it as brief as I can. Did you sleep much the night of the fire, Peggy, I mean before the fire started?'

'No.'

'Did you sleep at all? Even for half an hour that night?'

'No,' Peggy admitted slowly. 'I didn't sleep at all.'

'You were awake therefore when the fire started?'

'Yes, I suppose so,' Peggy mumbled.

'Lift your head, Peggy, so that we can hear,' Judge Masters said gently to her. 'It's rather difficult up here.'

'Yes, I suppose so!' Peggy said, lifting her head.

'Would you say that you would have known if someone had stolen into your house and set fire to it?'

'Yes. I suppose so.'

'*Did* anybody steal into your house that night and set it on fire?'

'No. Nobody did.'

'Are you sure, Peggy?'

'Yes of course I'm sure.'

'In other words you know that your father did not sneak in and set fire to the house that night.'

'Yes, I know he didn't.'

Strapp stood up and said: 'I don't think there can be anybody in this court, Your Honour, who doubts that statement ...'

My father was too cold now to be safe. 'I quite agree,' he said to Strapp. 'However, Peggy, you said that you would have known if anybody had set fire to that house ...'

'Yes.'

'Now, remembering your oath and your responsibility to your father here, do you know if anybody *did* deliberately set fire to that house.'

'Objection!' Strapp roared. 'It's the most heinous line of questioning of a young girl I have ever heard in my entire life.'

My father looked at Masters and knew the answer.

'You may proceed, Mr Quayle,' Masters said grimly, savagely, 'but I must say I don't like this at all.'

'Do you know, Peggy, if someone *did* deliberately set fire to your house?'

Peggy looked only at my father and knew already what was going to happen, long before anyone else knew except maybe Lockie himself and Mrs MacGibbon who was sitting in the public gallery tying her handkerchief in knots.

'Yes, I suppose I do know,' Peggy said.

Nobody could move or stir.

'Well? *Did* somebody, Peggy, set fire to your house or not?'

Strapp was on his feet and I thought he would lean over and swat my father with one of his pig paws. There was a violent and bitter argument. The point, however, was clear. Peggy was a material witness, this was a crucial question, the question itself was fair, the answer was necessary if this was to be cleared up, and she was clearly not being asked to incriminate her father.

'Allowed,' Judge Masters said, tight-lipped.

My father asked Peggy again. '*Did* somebody deliberately set fire to your house, Peggy?'

'Yes ...' Peggy said, two tears now breaking from her green eyes.

There was no uproar, there was no objection, we all knew we were watching a form of crucifixion by an impersonal God who formed the shape of a naked life, for this one moment, just the way he wanted it formed, and though there was pity and feeling and understanding and even compassion, there was something else that lived in this room that lived not outside it, something we must all settle here now or be damned forever. That was all in my father's back. I had long given up writing any of it down, Tom had long since lost his direction.

In the hollow, ticking silence my father asked the obvious next question: 'Then who did deliberately set fire to the house, Peggy?'

And before anyone could raise a protest Peggy put up one finger to stop one tear and said 'I did . . .'

My father had turned his back to Peggy as if he knew what would happen, and he was looking far down on Lockie sitting on the bench for the witnesses, and Lockie was looking at his daughter with tears streaming down his face, and I heard Mrs MacGibbon cry out: *'No, no, no. It's not true . . .'* Nobody else in the court seemed to know for a moment what had happened, as if only my father had really expected that self-incriminating answer; but looking back on it I wonder hopefully if he did know, because maybe he was also trying to prove that someone else was already in the house: not Lockie but Finn MacCooil or some other accessory. That was obviously what was in everybody else's mind as the questions had built up, including even Strapp and Judge Masters.

The whole case now disintegrated before our eyes.

My father managed one other ghostly question: 'And did your father know of this, Peggy?'

He knew it was a question that would never be allowed, but I think he wanted to take the weight off Peggy and put it on to Lockie. But Peggy would not answer it, which in itself was an answer, and Judge Masters was rapping on the wall behind him for order and Strapp was roaring protests and shouting at Peggy: 'You must not say anything more, Peggy, in your own interests. You must not answer any more questions, you are now incriminating yourself.'

The judge finally achieved some sort of silence with the help of the court police, and he looked down at my father with helpless anger: 'The behaviour of counsel in pursuing his questions in this manner has bordered on the unprincipled, and I can't help feeling that my original comment on your behaviour, Mr Quayle, was fully justified . . .'

But they were just words now, they went on, they didn't matter any more, nothing mattered. There was already nothing left of a lot of people in that court: not least Lockie and Peggy and Tom and me, and not least, not least at all, my father – who walked over to the table where Tom was hung up like a quartered sheep from a thousand invisible hooks in the sky. He took off his glasses and carefully folded up the briefs and tied them as the Judge ordered a recess, and he stood almost absent-mindedly beside Tom for a moment as if he wondered what all the fuss was about. He was quite removed. He was not my father, he was more like a man who had deliberately given away his heart to the four winds or to the gods of Olympus or to the empty sea: to something hopelessly outside us all.

Peggy's mother was hanging on to Peggy who dug her head into herself as deeply as she could, and when Tom got to her she broke away from her mother and clung to Tom who rubbed his head on her clipped hair like a friendly and gentle cat rubbing itself on a friendly and gentle arm or leg.

'It's all right, Peg,' he said in a stunned sort of way.

They pulled her away and I got a grip on Tom and they separated; and that seemed to be the end of an era for all of us.

Every judicial system in the world has its back rooms, and a great deal of backroom manipulation went on in the next few days. Judge Masters gave the only verdict possible in a closed court. Then Strapp saw to it that a case was brought quickly against Lockie and Peggy while sympathy for them was high, and it was dealt with in half an hour by Judge Masters without my father being present. They both pleaded guilty to a misdemeanour so there was no jury, and the facts were shifted a little so that Peggy's role in putting a torch to the house was reduced to something like an inspired accident, and Lockie's to gross negligence and misprision (concealing evidence).

Lockie was fined fifty pounds, and he gave a promise to the court that in view of Peggy's youth and honesty and good character he would take steps to see that she was never again exposed to such awful possibilities for tragic dishonour.

17

The steps that Lockie took should have been predictable, but even Tom did not anticipate everything happening so quickly.

Tom had simply gone to the bush across the Billabong to Burke's Crossing where he slept and spent the days wandering around the Billabong shooting hares and foxes, fishing and keeping as sane as he could.

It was Grace Gould who rang me at the *Standard* one morning and said: 'Did you know that Peggy MacGibbon was leaving by the mid-day train today?'

'Good God, no. Where to?'

'Castlemaine,' Grace said. 'But nobody is supposed to know.'

I didn't wait. Grace was a good girl. Being the station-master's daughter she had somehow found out about Peggy. I had to find Tom. I pedalled recklessly around to one of the Philby twins at the ironmonger's where he worked and begged him to lend me his motor-bike because I had to get to Tom, or at least to take me out there. Tod Philby resisted a while but finally he let me have it, although I was not expert on a motor-bike. Tod started the beautifully-kept old B S A for me and said: 'Now for Christ's sake, Kit, be careful. And use your clutch *with* the brake . . .'

I took off and went as fast as I dared through the town, simply hanging on as I roared down the metal road to the other bridge higher up the river. It was a flat little bridge, and on the other side there was a dirt road that wound through the wheat acreage and around the reedy swamps and by two or three deserted houses on the Billabong. I hoped that the iron gates which Shortlands (the owners of the Riverside acreage) sometimes kept locked were not locked today, and though I came close up to the closed gates, I could see the chain hanging loose. I leapt off the bike and opened the gates, got the bike through, closed the gates and fled along in my own wake of red dust towards Burke's Crossing, which was nothing more than an open patch of bush in a bend of the river.

Tom wasn't there, although his camp was.

I went back to the bike and blew the horn, one of those old mechanical horns which made a sickening rasping noise. I blew it a couple of times and then shouted. 'Tom . . . It's about Peggy . . . Where are you?'

I heard a rifle shot and saw Tom in one of the high reed beds, or rather just coming out of it. I waved urgently and he began to run towards me. I got on the bike and took it along a rough track as near as I dared, and when we met breathlessly I said:

'Listen. Peggy's leaving on the mid-day train.'

'Where to?'

'Castlemaine,' I said.

'Castlemaine! Oh, Christ,' he said desperately.

Neither of us had a watch but we could guess the time by the sun, and we knew we had very little time left. Tom got into the sidecar and I turned the bike awkwardly and sailed through my own dust again because it was still hanging listlessly in the hot morning air over the dusty track I had come on. Tom opened the gates, closed them, and we passed the houses, the bridge, and we were on the way down the main road at about sixty m.p.h. when Tom pulled on my shirt.

'We'll never make it,' he shouted. 'We're too late, Kit. Go down to the railway line.'

I swung off the road near an old orange grove and took a very bad track down to the level crossing, and even before I got there I could see the mid-day A3 pulling the long black and brown train. Tom leapt out and ran to the top of the cut near the crossing.

I couldn't see Peggy at first, but I knew she would be looking out somewhere. But on which side? It ought to be this side. The train was still within the town borders so there was still hope. Then I saw her and she saw Tom and stood up in her seat and began to pull at the window to get it down, gave up, and simply held her hands helplessly against the window and I could see her face pressed against the dirty glass in a frenzy. I could hear Tom shouting above the noise of the old A3 as he ran: 'Peggy, Peggy, Peggy . . .'

She was gone so quickly that Tom, running along the top of the bank, was shouting at nobody and at nothing.

We watched the train out of sight, and that was the last blow that could be dealt to Tom and Peggy by our town and our families and our violence and our bigotry and our narrow sense of narrow survival.

Peggy had gone to Castlemaine. That had only one meaning for all of us. Peggy had gone to become a nun at the Convent of the Sisters of Charity of St Vincent de Paul.

18

There is little left to tell about Tom and about Peggy, except what happened to them subsequently outside St Helen, although Tom was still in the town and had to survive a little longer in it.

He never went back to my father's office. My father and Tom had much more violent quarrels than before, always about politics, religion, honesty, truth, discipline, morality, law and the state of affairs we lived in; never about Peggy or Lockie or the town or the situation that had divided them forever. My father could not feel that he had done wrong, he had done what he had to do. Validity for him was correctly measured by its legal justification, nothing else, and no kind of contempt the town heaped on him had any kind of effect except to add to his own contempt for the Australian citizen and the Australian ignorance of what was right and what was wrong. God was God, the law was the law, my father was my father. They were three absolutes and I never tried to quarrel with any of them, not the way Tom did. Tom tackled them all and lashed my father into a fury.

I know that some Freudians like to interpret all human behaviour in an exclusively subjective colour – no whites, reds, blues or blacks, just grey the subjective colour. But I wonder if all Tom's behaviour was so subjective. It is true that overnight he gave up all measure of respect for the law and for my father (quite unjustifiably I think). It is also true that he naturally turned to old Hans Dreiser, and I think if it hadn't been for my mother he would have moved in with Hans.

But, objectively, Tom was ripe for what he was doing anyway. Maybe Peggy might have softened his attitude a little, but as the world began to take the first hesitant steps on the path it eventually took in September 1939 when we went to war with Hitler, there was already no other choice for hard, puritan Tom but to be serving his ideology properly: to set about doing what he knew he must do. Tom knew he would have to save the world before we knew it, and unknown to my father and mother Tom, now eighteen, went to the local high school and sat for an open examination for entry into the RAAF as an officer who would be trained to fly.

And that was not a subjective decision for Tom, I know it wasn't.

As usual on the twenty-fifth of April the Australian activity nearest to God, the Anzac parade, was held in the town. It always began with a fixed parade outside the Shire Hall. Then the local band played 'Recessional' which the town dignitaries, church men, farmers, lawyers, doctors, schoolmasters, shopkeepers and children sang like a national dirge. Then the old Anzacs of the town formed up and, led by Joe Collins the trooper in his trooper's outfit and with his medals clinking on his black breast as he danced dramatically on his mount, they marched by the town gardens and by the post office to the town square, where Tom and Hans Dreiser met them head on carrying two big placards.

'*1914–1918 was an Imperialist War!*' Hans Dreiser's placard said. '*Down with Imperialism.*'

'*No Appeasement of Hitler. Fight Fascism!*' Tom's said.

They looked like ants facing an elephant.

Joe Collins saw Tom like a man seeing a ghost he owed a bloody debt to, and he stabbed his spurs into his Gericault

mare and rode them both down in the righteous fury he felt
for their defilation of our military birthright and for Tom's
unmitigated gall in facing the whole town – particularly
Joe himself, mounted on his thoroughbred.

Tom went down like a baby. The horse reared and Tom
tried to fend it off with his placard and old Hans Dreiser was
trying to pull Tom free, but Joe had a dragon under his feet
and he lifted his horse several times and forced its prancing
black, polished hooves on Tom's legs and arms and anywhere
else. But Tom was agile, and though he took some bad blows
he hit Joe with the placard and it tore to shreds. Joe was
lashing out with his own feet and kicking at Tom who was
trying to pull him off the horse while old Hans, our Goethe
reader and revolutionary, was trying to pull Tom away
saying: 'Tom, Tom, no violence, Tom.' He shouted something in German at Collins, who swerved around and swearing and kicking his horse rode at Hans (the German) so that
Hans would have got the worst of it if four or five Anzacs
hadn't pulled them away. They lifted Tom off the road kicking and struggling.

'Get off that horse, you fascist,' Tom was shouting at
Collins as the Anzacs began to tear him apart. They were
either trying to restrain Tom or were trying to beat him to
pulp, I didn't wait to discover which was their main interest,
I fought my way to the footpath and dodged the boots and
the fists that were flying and got Tom to his feet and felt
someone hit my back, and I then saw Tom swinging right
and left and cursing the whole town, the stupidity of a town
that did not see eye-to-eye with him, any more than it saw
eye-to-eye with my father. Tom too would fight everything
and everybody at all times if necessary, and he was finally
delivered to the local foot constable, Pinky Ryan, who was
an old man who ground no axes, and I said to Tom 'Go with
him or they'll kill you, you bloody idiot.'

During all this time the band had not stopped playing what is now a famous tune – Colonel Bogey, and the march kept marching, and Joe, not to lose the one moment in his yearly life which he lived his entire life for, reined his lovely horse up and swung around and leapt like a trembling ballet dancer into the head of the parade again and it passed on thereafter in dignity and safety.

And that was Tom's last real meeting with the town of St Helen and all who lived in it.

19

Tom left the town two months later and it was reported another four months later that he had been seen outside the convent of The Sisters of Charity in Castlemaine, where he had obviously hoped to catch a glimpse of Peggy. But if he did go to Castlemaine Peggy did not know of it because she didn't see him, and when I heard of it I didn't believe it because the night before he left St Helen (when my mother had cooked a huge dinner for him which we had to walk off) I asked him point-blank about Peggy.

At the time I simply wanted to know what was in his mind and in his heart, and in that athletic young body which was now being prepared athletically for a war. I needed to know because I had watched the last golden glory of his youth disappear in the wake of Peggy's train, and though I don't think he had become embittered (he was still too young for that) he had overnight become a silent young man who seemed to be cutting part of himself off from the rest of us, as if he no longer trusted anyone absolutely, which meant that I no longer had any easy clues to what he was thinking.

So when I asked him about Peggy he simply ignored me, although I did get a hint of something. As we walked up the warm macadam road towards the cemetery he started to whistle to himself the Ravel *pavane* for the *infante défunte*, and I guessed then that in Tom's crystal-clear mind, which always needed a solution, Peggy was dead.

I am the romantic so I was a little shocked. I knew that if our medieval bush town had been living in its proper century I personally would have raided the convent and rescued the damsel. But Tom was not flimsy enough for that sort of imagination, and that was probably how he had survived the experience. He had buried Peggy as surely as if she had been dug into the earth with Dobey the Diver.

Which is why I didn't believe the story of Tom hanging around the convent of Castlemaine because it didn't fit him. By then he was in the RAAF anyway, learning to become a fighter pilot. Tom was, in fact, born to become a fighter pilot.

All the seeds of time that grew Tom now predicted his role. Everything he had been given put him into the air because he was born at the right time, almost to the second, nurtured perfectly in the world's best pastures for its prize animals, and brought up lovingly on milk and honey, and almost mathematically to the exact age when he could comprehend the huge machines he would hustle across the sky the way Joe Collins had hustled his Gericault horses across the sands of Gallipoli. The only trouble being that this perfect animal of the fighter plane, Tom, had something more besides.

He hated the RAAF. When he came home on leave in 1939, already a fully-fledged pilot about to fly Hawker Harts or Bristol Bulldogs or the kind of fighter planes the Australians had in those days, and when I asked him what the RAAF was like he said: 'They just beat your brains out. It's a stupid, wasteful business.'

'You mean you're sorry you did it?' I said in amazement.

'No. I had to do it,' he said calmly.

That was still Tom with a hard pure mind at work.

I was at home 'on leave' myself at the time, because I was about to take passage on a Norwegian cargo boat to England which old Mrs Royce had helped me to get work on through her son. She was giving up the paper and this was her bonus to me for some hard work. I left St Helen (and Australia) at about the same time Tom did, and I never saw Tom again.

Before we both left I did try once more to bring up with him the subject of Peggy and the MacGibbons, but by a clumsy route. I deliberately walked him down to Dog Island one night, and when we were sitting on the river bank I asked him: 'What do you think made Lockie come back that night?'

'I suppose he wanted to make sure his family were safe,' Tom said with a shrug. 'He hid in Somerfield's house and watched everything from there.'

'But when you think of it, Peggy was really risking her neck.'

'Of course she was risking her neck,' Tom said aggressively. 'Peggy had the guts to do anything. She would have set the whole town on fire if she had to.'

He was not being reluctant about Peggy, and for a moment I changed my guess about his fatalistic solution. Perhaps he had not buried Peggy after all but had rather accepted, like a betrayed lover, her marriage to someone else more immaculate than himself. After all he too had betrothed himself to an absolute inevitability. War, for Tom, was already an iron wife to whom he was tied hand and foot by moral conviction.

'Poor old Peg,' I sighed enticingly at the silver river.

But he did not open his mind again, not even a crack, so I failed for the last time to satisfy my sense of brotherly touch.

'We'd better go back,' he said.

He was thinking of his Manx mother, now trying to spare her as many more blows as he could. She was utterly lost over Tom and he knew it. My father had disciplined himself to go on being the normal Victorian English father. In fact he was still deeply puzzled by all the silent and angry fuss, although like Tom he was determined not to let it break him. But my mother felt everything through her skin, like me, and the shadow of Tom would never leave her, now or in the sad years yet to come.

'Okay, then,' I said as we got up. 'Let's go.'

We threw a couple of stones at Dog Island and listened to the bullfrogs and the quarrelling night-birds and fish plopping in the water and the faraway sound of someone laughing in the night, and then we went back home.

20

Tom was killed the following year on one of the first sorties he ever made. He had been sent to England to train on Hurricanes so that he could fly them with the RAAF when they eventually got them. He had volunteered to fly sorties with the RAF, and he was given permission to join 201 Squadron for three months and he took off one damp dawn in bad weather with three other Hurricanes to meet some returning Wellingtons which had been out night bombing and were coming back rather dangerously late in daylight.

Nobody ever knew what happened to him. The Hurricanes were over occupied Holland. There was no dramatic dog fight, no picture of Tom tearing apart the northern skies with his kangaroo leaps from star to star – his athletic sense of love. He simply disappeared in a badly organized rendezvous as far as any official view of it is concerned, and yet I know that he must have died by accident, by a bolt of lightning, by some fluke piece of metal which some German AA had fired at him, by some failure of a piston or a gasket or an oil pump or a connecting rod. Something failed him. He would never have failed his machine, and he would certainly have out-fought anything and everybody if he had the chance to, although you learn quickly in a war that you never do have the right kind of chance, not the measure of chance you feel is your due anyway. The bullet that kills you is simply a mistake in timing.

I had already been in the war myself. I had gone to Finland sensing trouble and happened to be there when the Russian-Finnish war started and I cabled a Melbourne paper and I never looked back. I remained in the war as a newspaperman, doing what I had always wanted and planned to do. But the poet dies hard and when I got the cable in Cairo from my sister telling me about Tom I wrote what is obviously a romantic view of aerial death:

> Clutched to one man's belly,
> The rigid brute of complex dynamos
> Is up to maul the air.
> There, upon another's heart,
> He holds the ghost's white hand,
> Is led upon the lakes of space,
> Is there when all the tents are gone.

It is not good, and I regret the glaring word *belly*, but it is as truthful an epitaph for Tom as anyone will ever write because nobody else will write one at all, as in fact no one really writes the proper death certificates for the victims of bad timing, or for the other breathers of life who come upon death deliberately because they are deliberately there. That is really the point I have tried to make clear about Tom. He was deliberately there; such people did exist.

In any case I had already seen too much death to feel one more pain, even if it came from my own nerve and my own body, which none of the others did. I had seen too many dead Russians in Finland, and dead Yorkshire clerks in Norway, and then dead dry Sicilians dead in their dead dry Mediterranean dust.

After Greece (where I met an English cousin in the RAF) I was back in Cairo when the last Australian contingent to be sent to the Middle East arrived at Suez. By now I was working for an English newspaper which had its own dignified role to play, and I had time to breathe before I wrote, time to feel so that I wrote what I felt, and because it wasn't a daily task but a rather irregular one I was never pressed, I was never meeting a deadline like most of my colleagues.

An Australian battalion or two was not much in terms of its approachable numbers, and when I had talked to some of the officers and some of the men, I went up to Ismailia where they were establishing a base hospital in an old Egyptian Army camp and I wandered into a low white store-room which had become a sort of canteen for the Australian nurses and started talking to some of them and laughing and joking and teasing with them, feeling so nostalgically at home for one second that I was not surprised when someone said to me in a very cheeky Australian voice:

'Hello, Kit. Fancy seeing you here.'

It was Peggy MacGibbon.

My surprise, my shock rather, was filled to the brim with stunned questions.

'But . . .'

Peggy MacGibbon had gone off to become a nun, we all knew that. *She had been taken out of life*, we all knew that too.

She laughed and said, 'You should see your face.'

'I'm sorry, Peg,' I said. 'But you'll have to forgive me.'

'What for?'

'I couldn't have imagined anyone I was less likely to meet.'

'Why?' Peggy said, teasing and provocative. 'What's so surprising about me being here.'

She knew all the questions that I needed to ask and to have answered, and she was not going to let me go until they were asked and answered, and she was also going to have a little devilish fun with me beforehand. I took her outside, and she said:

176

'I have to be back in half an hour, because we're having a dance. The Life Guards' band is in the next camp and they're coming over to welcome us.'

'You'll be back in time,' I said.

We went out on the desert and sat on one of the spit-and-polish stones, painted white, which formed a path around the hut. We overlooked the Canal, all around us was the hard sand of a very long and ancient land, which gave both of us a certain freedom of movement.

'Why aren't you a nun?' was my first and most obvious question.

'I was a novice on yearly vows and doing nursing in St Vincent's. But I asked to be released.'

'Why?'

'I can't tell you why, Kit.'

'Why not? What happened?' I persisted, remembering too clearly Tom's last effort to catch her.

'Nothing happened. I don't even want to think about it, so don't ask me.'

'You don't mean you lost your religion?'

'Of course not. How can you say such a thing. It's just something better left unsaid and unthought of. Please! It's funny how different you look in uniform. Me too, I suppose. But I had forgotten how tall and thin you were, how unlike Tom you were.'

'You must have heard about Tom.'

'Smilie wrote me,' she said.

People don't break their hearts in public and don't even crack them or cut them open or pour out a drop of blood or even reveal a scar. If strong they bleed, and they bleed internally, so I suppose Peggy must have dropped some of her precious heart into some youthful chalice when I mentioned Tom, drop by drop, but I didn't see it.

'I wept a lot,' she said, but almost as an afterthought.

'He didn't know, did he, that you were not in Holy Orders . . .?'

'No,' she said. 'But I didn't know either that he was going to die so soon,' she added so simply that it explained a great deal.

'Well I'll be damned anyway,' I said, quite pleased with my own naked pleasure.

I took her hand, she laughed and tucked her hand into my arm and we walked towards the Canal which was more like a dark blue stain on the back of the night than a sheet of fake water, neither of one sea nor the other.

'How's the rest of the family?' she asked me. 'I mean your father and mother and Jeannie?'

'They're all right,' I said. 'Jeannie will become a doctor after all. The war now makes everything possible. How's *your* family?'

'The same,' she said. 'Lockie's going to be rich, for a while anyway. They're opening an RAAF training base at Nooah on the salt lake and he's gone up there to open a cinema.'

We had ironed out our lives in two or three sentences: no bitterness, no hatred, no recollections that had to be annihilated. We had already annihilated everything, both of us, and I suddenly stopped her and took a good glance at her because so far she had been more a presence than a living person.

She was not the same Peggy because she couldn't be. Take a look at Peggy with green eyes and red hair and faint freckles she had tried all her life to wash out with lemon, vinegar, creams and failed to, and see her in sandy blue light under more white stars than seemed possible to cram into one arc of the sky. See that Peggy and not feel affected.

'What a funny bloke you always were,' she said.

'Don't say bloke,' I told her, feeling robbed of her perfection.

'Don't be silly,' she said, instantly tough with me. 'That's what you are. What else are you?'

'It's a clumsy word coming out of your mouth,' I said firmly.

She laughed. 'Do you still write poetry?' she mocked.

'No!' I said angrily. 'Who told you I ever did?'

'Grace Gould.'

'Great God Almighty. Don't women ever keep secrets?'

Some drunken Australian soldiers, some drunken English soldiers, were doing a jig in our path as we neared the Canal, and the shouting and drunken songs and the nerveless bodies of folded men were suddenly too near for comfort.

'Let's go back,' I said.

'Why?' Peggy said. 'They won't hurt you.'

'How do you know they won't?' I said. 'I was thinking of you.'

'You were always afraid of the boys on Dunlap Street when they were drunk. I used to watch you.'

Peggy, I remembered, had watched everything with those tempting eyes, even me.

We walked on, Peggy keeping a firm grip on my arm as if to guide me and steer me through trouble, and she said: 'Don't you realize that a man who is drunk is like a dog. If you show you are afraid of him he becomes aggressive, if you're not afraid of him and ignore him then he ignores you, or rather he doesn't want to beat you up.'

We marched through the Dunlap Street of this fine old country and safely reached the water on a sandy strip where I had to hold Peggy as she slid down the gentle bank. When we stood by the water she sat down and pulled off one brown shoe and one brown stocking and put her foot into the Canal and said: 'That's a baptism! Catholics love all baptismal rites,' and she borrowed my handkerchief, dried her foot, put her stocking back on and her shoe and said: 'Come on, you can come back to the dance with me ...'

We went back through the drunken soldiers, and though I believed Peggy was right about showing them a bold face I knew it was a fake face with me but a genuine one with her. After all Peggy was the girl who always had the courage. Peggy was the girl who had set fire to her own house, Peggy was the girl who had put her heart publicly at Tom's feet, Peggy was the girl who had climbed out of a locked house to find Tom – twice, and Peggy was the girl who, faced with that demon in his own court and in his own private world, had refused to tell a lie to a man who only expected the truth from her, suicidal as it was.

'Your hair ...' I said involuntarily, because (as I must repeat) I live my feeling and I was living three lives in one recollection.

She had an Australian Army nurse's uniform hat on and she took it off and shook her head, and out flew her short red flames licking me so faintly. They were so ghostlike that I almost shrunk back.

'My God, Peggy ...' I said, overwhelmed.

'What?' she said calmly.

But she knew *what*. She knew.

21

I married Peggy, or rather the Roman Catholic Chaplain of the AIF's 2nd Base Hospital married us, eight months and four days exactly after we had met that night at Ismailia. I married Peggy in her full baptismal name – Margaret Eileen Mary MacGibbon and the day we were married she said to me: 'I don't want you to call me Peggy ever again. Never. Call me Eileen or Mary.'

'But that's absolutely ridiculous,' I protested. 'You can only be Peggy to me.'

'No, Kit,' she said seriously. 'I mean it. Please! Eileen or Mary: take your pick. But no more Peggy.'

It was the first of many fragments we would spend time smashing into smaller fragments. Peggy had bled and was still bleeding – maybe not for Tom who was dead, but for all that damage, all that pain, all that unsolved flow of life that had stopped flowing. I was tactful enough then to agree and be gentle with her, but in the years that followed I was not always as tactful because sometimes I had to crack an old mirror she sometimes unconsciously held up to me of a dead boy – one I wanted her to forget and yet did not want to forget myself.

'I never touched Tom, I mean immorally, nor did Tom ever touch me that way,' she shouted at me once in a fury when we were quarrelling about love. 'If Tom and I had ever been anything but pure and innocent with each other I would never have married you at all. I wouldn't have even *touched* you.'

I knew that I had loved Peggy for a long time without deliberately loving her and without acknowledging the thought even to myself except in some subliminal flash that would destroy itself even when it passed through my mind. I too had been pure in thought in that respect. Admittedly I had imagined that I had been in love with others: once in Finland with a Swede, once in Cairo with a beautiful Armenian girl, once in Alexandria with a sad Jewish girl with pale, pale eyes. But there never was a dream so rare whose reality did not thrive on a second chance.

Before we were married, when I would come back from some stint in the Western Desert or some turn with the fleet or some bombing raid with Blenheims, I would find Peggy with a ripe heart waiting as if death mattered to her. And one more death *would* matter to her. Mine. That was our courtship. I was shamelessly playing on a tragic lyre. I used it recklessly. I would ring her up and tell her when I was going off and tell her when I would be back, always planning my return far too early, and I would not come back on time, I would be delayed, I would be sunk in some jewel of a sea or dead in some spiritless air or rotting on some faint far hill of treeless sand.

When I did come I was met by Peggy in agony. I was devoured with passionate embraces and a stupefying, clinging flow of nerves to my nerves from which there seemed to be no parturition. We were in love in fear of another disintegration, and this time we had a good measurer permanently affixed to us to record the nearness of disaster. War is what serves love best and with most passion, because the price you pay for it is permanently obvious.

We had difficulties. When we married she was ordered home, but I had my own way of fighting and I fought and she remained, technically as a nurse in a civil hospital, but she did nothing that served more than her sense of moral duty insisted on. She was too terrified for me. I was shifted to Moscow in 1942 and for a Catholic girl that could have been a frightening experience and it began the six years of moral fighting between us which was happy and fierce and tangled up in worlds at play and worlds spinning confusion around us. I fought, Eileen fought. We postponed anything more (children) until we had settled what we were. No day passed without that passionate dispute which would settle the world between us, because the day Tom died I had deliberately (and perhaps romantically) taken up his role and I had tried to become the hard puritan, believing in a destiny which I could serve and a future which was far beyond the limits of religion, family and work. I had learned to believe in some remarkable and unexploited future as passionately as Tom had. And Eileen, by sheer visual pressure, by an experience which crushed thousands of old prejudices out of her life every day (only to have them returned again at night when she lay awake in some dark room, afraid of herself, her God, her conscience, her future), Eileen discovered that the world was won not with faith and not with fear but by the serious efforts of the victim himself.

Actually God was never an issue between us, yet in some ways Eileen has been more afraid of the God she says she no longer believes in than she ever was of the one she did believe in. Our problem was not a sectual one either, it was simply the remnants of our dangerous and unexploded past that went on dividing us for so many years.

Yet I look back on what happened between Lockie and my father and between Tom and my father and between Tom and Peggy and I only see it now as an almost national predestination for Peggy and myself. Australia has had a history of peculiar impositions: of authority (English) on the one hand, and of rebellious peasants (Australians) on the other. Peggy and I are its logical children. My father was no more really than a moral governor of a convict settlement bearing Magna Carta with him, and Lockie was no more than a free man who had broken out of some far-away Magna Carta prison and would never submit again to the rules that meant so much to those who ruled him.

The division was even, but I think behaviour was in Lockie's favour. He knew how to act as a man. Yet Lockie was so ignorant that his outlook was medieval, and his only yardstick for life was a rigorous and childish dogma. My father's outlook, despite its stupidities, had a wider field for a man to survive in, and Peggy and I had to fight that out, because she and Tom had avoided fighting it out. We had to marry our differences, and emerge somehow from them.

I can say these things now, at the end of this story of Tom and Peggy because I feel, after twenty years of exile from our sacred river, that they need to be said, not simply to explain a love story but because Australians don't say them yet. What Australians haven't so far looked for in themselves is their own personality and where it has really come from. Perhaps they are too near to it to see it. Their literature has not helped them, because it perpetuates the myth of the outback Australian who doesn't really exist any more. Diggership, Anzacship, good-on-youship is no explanation. The boundary rider even less. But what happened in a small town like St Helen between Lockie and my father, between Peggy and Tom, between Finn MacCooil and his fighting fists, between the river and Dobey and Charlie Castle and his leap and the hundreds of other men in any town in our island continent is what makes the startling Australian character what it is, although so far it is unspoken of.

I only touch it delicately with my fingertips here, because I am no longer part of it. I prefer the memory to the reality because I know that if I ever went back I would die of one more touch of it, so I live in England as an exile from the haunts of that one cold touch. Neither Peggy nor I want to go back although we long sometimes for our perfect rivers, our drip-dry trees, our bush birds talking like Cockneys, and the Harbingers of Spring which push their little golden bells barely above the earth in *our* spring which comes upside down in September and October. But I never want to see our town of St Helen again, and I never want to touch its ignorance, its intolerance or its religious stupidity, or the egalitarian bludgeoning of its Australian mockery.

But I think that if Tom had lived he would never have left Australia. He would have gone back to it and lived out his life there doing the kind of thing he had set himself to do, and he would have done it well. His hard sense of purpose and his unashamed desire to do right would have been a useful morality now. *I* think so; and that is what I have tried to bring to my own son. Eileen would not even name our son (who was born in the seventh and most peaceful year after we married) with any name from our families, friends or acquaintances. She insisted again on starting anew, so we began with Dick. We *have* been back once to St Helen before there were children, just after the war, and I sat with Lockie and Mrs MacGibbon over a cup of tea one night and Lockie said to me: 'I never heard of you fighting anybody in this town, Kit. I suppose that's what made you into a scribbler.'

I laughed, because maybe he was right.

I watched Eileen overcome her profound fear of my father and walk around behind him when he was working in the garden, talking to him the way an affectionate daughter-in-law should talk to an ageing father-in-law, and though I always felt that my father found some slight moral wrong in our marriage, none the less there was no more war in that town between the Quayles and the MacGibbons; there was simply an end.

Neither family has seen Dick or our bubbling daughter Kate. They never will. Dick is like Eileen, Kate is a little like me but sometimes she is startlingly like Tom, and I see Eileen soaping her in the bath or rubbing her wet hair with a towel and hanging on, suddenly, for one moment, to some unquenchable memory. Peggy doesn't weep for Tom any more, because she is now Eileen. But she is always afraid that she will have to weep for her son, and what I have tried to do here is record another kind of morality of another kind of boy who had only the highest hopes. He wanted to save the world, and he really did die trying to do it.

So for Eileen's sake I dedicate this book not to Tom but to my children, hoping that they will try, as Tom did, to overcome the impoverishment of their generation, the awful bigotry of dead morals, the violence of violent systems, and the corruption of a life lived without meaning. If they will try to see life nobly then I know Eileen will never have to weep for her son, as she once wept for my brother, Tom.

Also by James Aldridge

The True Story of Lilli Stubeck

When the down and out Stubeck family arrived in the Australian country town of St Helen no one expected that they would stay for long; nor, when they left, that it would be without their daughter Lilli.

It was a mystery, too, why wealthy Miss Dalgleish should 'buy' the wilful girl and try to tame her, for Lilli was fiercely determined never to be anyone but Lilli.

With a battle of wills for possession of her soul, and with the unexpected return of her scavenging family, what did the real future hold for Lilli?

The True Story of Spit MacPhee

The people of St Helen are concerned for young Spit MacPhee who lives a hand-to-mouth existence with his eccentric grandfather down by the river.

Certainly life is tough, but Spit is a natural boy in a natural landscape and he accepts things for the way they are. Although his relationship with old Fyfe is one of unquestioned understanding and sharing, it appears to outsiders that Spit is left to his own devices.

When his grandfather dies, Spit faces the tragedy with typical determination, but the well-intentioned townsfolk seize the opportunity to intervene – to them the boy is a vagabond needing protection and guidance. Spit finds himself hunted by his benefactors and eventually the subject of a dramatic court case which polarises the religious and moral attitudes of a typical Australian country town in the 1930s. Yet such is the strength of young Spit's character that as the truth about his life with old Fyfe is revealed, no one is left unchanged.

Also available in Penguin

Harland's Half Acre
David Malouf

A story rich in passion and incident and with the obsessive, sometimes violent claims of family life.

From his poverty-stricken upbringing on a dairy farm in Queensland, Frank Harland nurtures his artistic genius until the time comes when he can take possession of his dreams.

Inextricably tangled with Frank is Phil Vernon, the only child of a wealthy Brisbane family, whose roots stretch back to England.

Together their voices echo the story of a great country in a novel of remarkable artistry and power.

Johnno
David Malouf

With a poet's eye for the fine detail, David Malouf has written a rare, sparkling evocation of an Australian boyhood in the forties, of the pubs and brothels of the fifties, and the years away overseas. An affectionately outrageous portrait, *Johnno* brilliantly recreates the sleazy tropical half-city that was wartime Brisbane and captures a generation locked in combat with the elusive Australian Dream.